Edited by Douglas Glover

Best Canadian Stories
99

This book was published with the assistance of the Canada Council and others. We acknowledge the support of the Canada Council for the Arts and the Government of Canada through the Book Publishing Industry Development Program for our publishing activities. Canadä

Acknowledgements: "Napoleon in Moscow" by Matt Cohen and "My Romance" by Douglas Glover were first published in *Descant.* "Goombay Smash" by Jane Eaton Hamilton originally appeared in *Prism International.* "Four Days from Oregon" by Madeleine Thien was originally published in *Fiddlehead.* "Karaoke Mon Amour" by Mike Barnes and "Three Weeks" by Libby Creelman will appear in *The New Quarterly.*

The following magazines were consulted: *The Antigonish Review, Blood & Aphorisms, Canadian Author, Canadian Fiction Magazine, Canadian Forum, The Capilano Review, Descant, Event, The Fiddlehead, Geist, grain, Malahat Review, The New Quarterly, The New Yorker, Nimrod, Paragraph, Prairie Fire, Quarry, Saturday Night* and *Windsor Review.*

ISBN 0 7780 1124 0 (hardcover)
ISBN 0 7780 1125 9 (softcover)
ISSN 0703 9476

Cover art by Mendelson Joe
Book design by Michael Macklem

Printed in Canada

PUBLISHED IN CANADA BY OBERON PRESS

Contributions for the thirtieth volume, published or unpublished, should be sent to Oberon Press, 400–350 Sparks Street, Ottawa, Ontario KIR 7S8 before 31 January, 2000. All manuscripts should enclose a stamped self-addressed envelope.

I PICK THESE stories myself. It's very subjective. No apologies. Every anthology is autobiographical—and the subject is the editor. Maybe this goes without saying (and, like most truisms, isn't actually true). All the stories in this year's collection are about lost love, cracked love, broken dreams, and nostalgia (I turned 50 last November—what else is there to think about?). All except for Bruce McCall's gorgeous parody "The Hidden Life of Doges" which is about, well, a man's love for his doge. I've been seeing McCall's cartoons and humour pieces in *The New Yorker* for years, but then I read his melancholy yet defiant 1997 memoir *Thin Ice*, about growing up in southern Ontario in the forties and fifties, and realized what an ardent, tortured and quintessential Canadian he is.

This year I did not find much to love in the magazines. Don't know why—bad weather in the Prairies? funding cutbacks and a failure of editorial nerve? El Niño? Yes, in *Descant* there was Matt Cohen's "Napoleon in Moscow," the sad, lovely, mordantly witty story of a real-estate agent who thinks he's Napoleon Bonaparte and a doomed, bittersweet reunion with his estranged wife. "It is easier to conquer a country than a heart. Napoleon said that. Or perhaps it was me. It's amazing what I can come out with, mostly by accident." And, again in *Descant*, my own story "My Romance," a shocking meditation on love, language, and the death of a child. "Our boy Neddy died when he was three months old. I hardly remember any of this except for the brief hours following his birth when we were a normal, happy couple and then afterwards when Annie would wake in the night, choked with sobs, her milk streaming through the cloth of her nightgown. 'My baby is hungry. He needs to eat,' she would whisper." And, in *Prism International*, Jane Eaton Hamilton's comically bittersweet lesbian romance "Goombay Smash"—"you have lain nude on your car, a gigantic hood ornament, in your garage that smells of dirty oil, waiting for her to arrive home, and raise the door with her remote." But after these, I had to pan for gold in the slush pile and shake the editorial tree for unpublished work.

In upstate New York I found François Bonneville, a transplanted French-Canadian who writes stories like "The Sky-Coloured Boat," a syntactic fusion of baroque Latinate exuberance and stern American minimalism. In Vancouver, I found Adam Lewis Schroeder's "Balinese," a strange, enigmatic tale about art, sexual obsession and lost letters set in World War II Bali. "Then it flitted through Potgieter's mind what a fine painting this scene would make, so full of colour and activity, the Balinese all in yellows and reds, the Japanese in their uniforms of drab beige, the dogs and children scrambling around everyone's knees, the morning light glancing off the bayonets and the windshield and playing across the faces of the crowd, the soldiers, himself." And Madeleine Thien's "Four Days from Oregon," the sad story of a girl, walking wounded, permanently torn between a crazy mother, her lost, ineffectual father and the kindly, long-suffering stepfather she cannot learn to love.

In Toronto, I found Mike Barnes, a poet-turned-story writer whose "Karaoke Mon Amour" is a complex mirror image of the Schroeder story: a Toronto man yearns for the mysterious, lively Oriental women to whom he teaches English while a sterile relationship with his Anglo lover disintegrates. And finally in Newfoundland, I found Libby Creelman and her delightful story "Three Weeks"—a sweltering amalgam of summer heat, adolescent sexuality, dope and loneliness written in a prose style as limpid and precise as a clear pool yet full of a restless, original energy. "Then he moved his fingers around one of her thighs, then the other, thoughtfully and with his face averted like a person picking a raffle ticket from a hat, and untangled her underwear. Despite some distant, dreary mortification, she waited to see if he would pull them up."

DOUGLAS GLOVER

Napoleon in Moscow

Matt Cohen

I

Napoleon is dead and everyone wants to know. How did it happen? Was it death by poison, from the boredom of exile, at the hand of a last absurd campaign to build a last futile empire? Napoleon is dead, but I prefer to remember Napoleon in his days of glory, Napoleon at his most mysterious. Napoleon in Moscow.

We are in the square outside his winter palace. Stella's excited breath tickling my ear as she clutches my arm and we kick our booted feet in the thick snow. Above us, Napoleon's window, heavy with golden candlelight, glowing into the dark night the way our naked skin glows against the thick surrounding pelts.

While the moon recovers from last night's eclipse, snow falls hard from the sullen sky. Otters lie dreaming in their river-bank homes, their dark fur shines with the fish eyes they have eaten. On the lonely road that passes by my cabin, a snowplough moans, its blue revolving light flashes through my window and across the room. Snow swirls and beats against the window. I am Napoleon in Moscow. My soldiers occupy the squares and swarm through the twisted streets in search of food. Nothing you hide will be safe from me.

I am listening to Japanese music. I am trying to make sense of my life. But I'm not some kind of heavy thinker. Far from it. My plan is to get the life problem structured, then carry on the way I used to, your normal greedy, selfish, manic-depressive person.

What I'm looking for now is a new master plan. I always used to have goals. For example, when I was a real-estate salesman, which in a half-hearted way I still am, my goal first expressed itself in the number of houses I sold. After a while I dropped the pretence and it was just a matter of making a certain amount of money. Excuses: wife, children, mortgage, etc. I'm not talking anything fancy, though I admit I started wanting appliances.

I am opposed to the concept of appliances. What about guillotines you will ask? We'll come to that later. The Empire banned appliances by decree. Loyal patriots were in danger of destroying their lives by allowing themselves to desire dishwashers, trash compactors, ice-cube-generating refrigerators. Even microwaves and hair-dryers could poison more than the soul. That was my position and I inscribed it in the code. It sounds foolish, but it worked. Firstly, it allowed me to feel superior to most people, which made up for the fact that most people feel—quite rightly in my opinion—superior to me. Secondly, the hours spent walking around with my head in a towel washing dishes, defrosting, percolating coffee, etc., etc., gave my life a certain shape. A structure. Since I'm currently looking for a new structure you might wonder why I don't return to the old.

The old life was Stella. The children. The nights we spent trying to make the numbers balance. Afterwards, but not always, we would go upstairs and balance on each other. Even on a night such as this, with the snow falling heavy and the revolving blue light of the snowplough like a searchlight sweeping our white bellies.

I am Napoleon in Moscow. "Napoleon in Moscow!" Stella laughed. This was after she had left, not necessarily forever, just a "trial separation" as she said, a holiday during which she would take the children and stay in town with her sister whose house was too big anyway—guess who sold it to her! —and since then, to tell the truth, the trial has been dragging on.

"That's me," I said, "Napoleon in Moscow."

"How do you know?"

"Demons called me on the telephone. I thought it was some kind of police association lottery. But they insisted. 'How can I be sure?' 'Look at your right hand.' I took my hand out of my jacket where I had been, by coincidence, believe me, scratching my stomach. The word 'Napoleon' appeared on my palm."

"I think you're letting yourself go," Stella said.

As Napoleon I face a different configuration. I could lie on Stella and use her body to trace out my campaigns. Slit trenches, guided missiles, raiding parties, submarine attacks. But Napoleon was more interested in snow. That is why he had his men die there, rather than while making love with their loved ones.

2

My deeds will be recorded. Museums will rise in my name. The earth will be torn apart, shovels and pickaxes wielded in a chorus louder than any marching band to extract the lead from which millions of toy soldiers will be made in my image. Small boys the world over will turn me in their fingers. They will marvel at the splendour of my uniform, the bizarre cannonball shape of my head, the way I keep one hand warm by holding it inside my jacket. "Napoleon," those young voices will whisper in the night. The way my soldiers have always whispered my name. In the night. Full of admiration, dread and wonder at the—why does he do it? they ask themselves, who is it winds up this tiny conquest machine? With what light burns that brain which keeps inventing ways to raise and then exhaust armies on the world's battlefields? Etc.

The truth is, I have no answers. First I created the Empire, then the Empire created me. World history is a ping-pong match between my inscrutable unstoppable self and the marvels that self has created. And I? The *moi* behind the mask? Just another orphan soul tossing on the seas of destiny, even though those seas move to the tides I myself have caused.

The truth is that like all great French generals and statesmen, I am a man of action by default. My real vocation was to be a writer but my early stories were rejected by corrupt monarchist editors who wished to suppress the truth about Corsica. Before they went to the blade, my poems were taped to their mouths. Now I feel most myself in the night-silence of my tent, the candles sputtering, the white paper stretches out in creamy reams softer than the eyeball of an Empress. My letters to Josephine, my diaries of war, but most of all the words unwritten, the vast armies of prose I would send marching across untold pages—those unwritten armies that have sunk into the whiteness of paper like my troops into the snow of the endless Russian plains.

Lost, yes, because how can words convey the splendour of these pre-dawn hours, the wonder of being alone in a tent nearby tomorrow's battlefield. Outside my canvas the starry sky sparkles over the heads of my sleeping troops, 400,000 men lurching toward the dawn, toward the first light that will jerk them awake, full of fear and hunger and that wild chaos only I can harness, only I can turn into an orderly hurricane of violence that will send them flying into the enemy, hacking and being hacked until their skins split, their bones shatter, their blood masses in stinking pools slowly draining to dark patches on the earth so at the end of the day, as the sun sets on the dead and the dying, as the cries of the wounded rise above the surgeons' saws and the hasty whispered prayers of my priests, I, Napoleon, repulsed, sated, sick at heart, fulfilled, I will mourn that great unconscious mass of men who sleep around me now; I will mourn their dead and crippled horses, their orphans, the rivers of wine they will never drink, the ageing flesh their hands will never know. Monster, yes, that is the title with which history will reward me, but I am most at home in my lonely simple tent, doing the job that has been left to me, the manufacture of dreams and nightmares, sending my word-rich armies onto their pages of snow, letting them cancel and slaughter each other until all that remains is a brief and elegant poem, a few nostalgic blood-tinted lines limping toward eternity, yes, that's how I want to be remembered, bleeding and limping in rags across the snow, or even forget the blood, the rags, the snow, the limp. Just me.

3

When the blackness of night expands blue and yellow, I step outside and strap on my skis. At this hour snow creaks. Branches snap. My troops stir amongst the leafless ghostly poplars that rise with the sun from the snow, arch their frozen branches into the cold liquid light pouring up from the eastern horizon. A few strides and the cabin is behind me, the pale hint of a lantern, a whiff of woodsmoke, then nothing at all as I glide into the soft belly of my marsh, coast down into the dark piney bush that waits to embrace me.

4

My bucking Bronco bucks and bronks. My 286-horse cavalry moans, then roars and whinnies beneath the snow-covered hood, white stuff flies in all direction as we power our way toward the road, leaving behind us the great rutted tracks of our charge.

The empire of the sun is back. Its weak light shines through veils of swirling snow, low half-convinced clouds that lie crouched along the horizon. The black asphalt of the highway has been scraped clean. The school buses have already passed to pick up their roadside cargoes of ski-jacketed children, now all that remains in front of each house is its pile of lopsided green garbage bags and blue-recycle boxes, waiting for the big yellow township trucks.

On the way to my office I pass the dump. Despite last night's snow, the air is still and clearing. They're having a little burnoff, smoke rises straight and orderly toward the washed-out dome of the sky. The dump is where I open my thermos. I love the way the steam rises into my face, the bittersweet coffee scalds my waiting tongue.

Twenty minutes later and I'm at my office, a cube in a plaza off the main highway. Frank has been and gone. The office smells of baseboard heaters, wet wool, prehistoric pizza crusts. When the red light starts blinking I pick up the phone. It's Stella, unusually.

"You all right?"

"Of course."

"Frank said...."

"Frank called you?"

"Last night, of course, after...."

Last night after work Frank and I went to Aunt Lucy's, grabbed something to eat in the sports bar. Frank is always going for the nachos, pure grease, but even if it is crazy to worry about vegetables I like a plate of crunchies with the cheese dip. Then a hamburger. Not exactly a health-spa special but at least the kind of meal you could admit to your doctor. A few beers and then, again maybe this is crazy too, but after a certain number it's not that good for you so I switch to scotch and water. At least you know what you're

14

getting and where you are.

Last night after the switch I told Frank, nothing intended, that his face was starting to look like the nachos he was eating, tomato red with yellow stuff bubbling around the edges. "Look at your nose," I now remembered saying, Stella's silence bringing it all back, "one big glob of pepperoni."

"I didn't mean to hurt his feelings," I told Stella.

"He fired you," Stella said.

We'd been yelling in the parking-lot and then Frank had screamed something about my not coming back. I'd picked him up by the coat, not really meaning to hurt him. That was when he'd let me have it in the face. Wouldn't have thought he could. Left me there my nose spouting like a hydrant.

"Wanted me to call and apologize for him. Ask you to come back."

"Here I am."

"Well I'm here," Stella said.

"The kids at school?"

"That's right."

A questioning silence settled in. Stella's sister was in Florida. The kids were gone for hours. My nose was fine and I had my job back. "You hoping for a visit?"

"*Hoping?*" Stella repeated, giving the word a half-twist and just enough vinegar to let me know she could have drowned it if she wanted to.

I put my hand in my jacket. I'd lost the opening skirmish, but as every general knows, you can't win a battle unless you manage to engage the enemy.

"Well," I said, sounding a half-note of defeat and withdrawal. "I'm out of coffee," Stella said. "You could pick some up on the way."

It is easier to conquer a country than a heart. Napoleon said that. Or perhaps it was me. It's amazing what I can come out with, mostly by accident, when I've had an extra cup of coffee or a few glasses of scotch and a few thousand brain cells are tipped into mass suicide, the sound of their explosion filling my skull like the celebration of so much overheated popcorn. Stella of course, Stella doesn't appreciate these little dictums. She doesn't want to play Josephine to my Napoleon. "Well, then, you can be my Stella," I once offered her, but she didn't realize what I meant, she never takes the long view, Stella, the backwards glance from the future that allows us to know what we're going through is just so much history waiting to be corrected by a little makeup, various lies and omissions, various inventions pointless to try to guess in advance. She thinks, to put it bluntly, that what's happening right now is some kind of "reality." I do my best to adjust, pretend, sometimes even try to convince myself, but in the end I'm back to the long view, the realization Stella is but one of a number of campaigns, a point, perhaps even the high point, of my life-to-be with her as-yet-unencountered successors. "Stella," I'll one day sigh, possibly with the same bitter regret and loss I often feel for her even now. She'll have forgotten me. She'll be in some new present, some new "reality." Her life with me will be summed up by a few pictures in an album and the odd memory that catches her unexpectedly in the ribs.

We start off in the kitchen. To show goodwill I myself put the water in the kettle, though my hands begin to tremble and it spills before I can even get it to the stove. "You might as well come upstairs," Stella then says, not unkindly.

I follow her up. She's wearing a soft white sweater of wool so fine I can't imagine it between my fingers, dark pants stretched tight over the bum I also want to touch. While I sit on the edge of her sister's bed Stella goes into the bathroom to undress, then comes back in her white terrycloth robe, the one I bought her last Christmas.

We climb in. In the morning winter light our skin is grainy, helpless. Soon we're under the sheets, humping and groaning. Do we love each other or are we just condemned to this weird sweet need? Afterwards we're lying side by side, and I'm looking up at my sister-in-law's pink stuccoed ceiling wondering if she too has inspected this dubious touch in the afterglow of sex, and then the whole need comes on us again. This time, hovering above Stella, I open my eyes and look down on her. Her white legs are spread in a perfect V, and I suddenly remember when Crystal was born: just before the final contractions Stella was lying this way, her legs splayed, exhausted, then suddenly her knees jerked up, Stella's face and throat turned scarlet, her huge belly banded with muscle and effort—

In the shower my nose starts to bleed again. To save the towels I stand above the sink, holding toilet paper to my face. When I come back into the bedroom Stella is lying where I left her, hands clasped behind her head, making her own study of the pink stucco.

"You could stay for supper," Stella says.

I want to see the children. I want Stella. I want to slip into this pink stucco cocoon and sleep away my life until I come out dead on the other side.

But there's something in this I can't do. I can't burden the brightness of their living with the awkward shadow of my death, of my long view in which after all the dazzling campaigns, the retreats, the exiles, the empires constructed out of countries not yet named, the years spent in dungeons not yet built, I'll be lying in the ground somewhere and they'll be standing over me, not sure whether to weep or just be relieved.

"Don't make it into a big thing," Stella says.

I sit down on the edge of the bed. Outside the snow is sheeting against the windows. "Look at it," I say.

Stella pulls the sheets and covers up to her neck. "At least you could bring me some of the coffee you promised."

"I also got some wine."

"The corkscrew's in the drawer beside the fridge."

17

Soon all the windows are plastered with snow. We're plastered too, not really, just dizzy with all the times we keep going back to Stella's sister's bed. By the time we make it down to the kitchen, more or less dressed, to find something to eat, it's mid-afternoon and according to the radio, the highways and the schools are closing.

When school lets out we're both there. Crystal and Robbie have their scarves wrapped round their faces, the snow is blowing into everyone's eyes, we stagger into my bucking Bronco and drive the few blocks home without anyone doing anything but clapping their hands and panting.

I help Crystal, who is seven, out of her snowpants. She looks at me curiously at first, it's been weeks, then just goes along as if everything is normal, as if I've been here every night for the past several months kissing her beet-red cheeks, helping her in and out of clothes, reading her stories while she waits for her bath. Robbie, five, stays in the circle of his mother's arms, watching suspiciously. But when I pick him up he throws his arms around my neck, then presses his face into my chest so hard that it hurts.

When all the coats and boots are piled up they run off to the family-room I was so careful to point out to Carrie when she bought the house. Sprawled out on the apricot shag wall-to-wall that was featured in the ad, they watch the big colour television Carrie's husband Cal bought for the Stanley Cup a few years ago. Stella and I can see them from the kitchen. While she makes hot chocolate I look in the freezer and cupboards. "I'll do spaghetti," I announce, as if about to distribute a *cordon bleu* meal to my troops stranded knee-deep on the Russian steppes.

"Great," Stella says. "A night off cooking. That calls for another bottle of wine."

The house I sold Carrie is warm. There's real central heating, a gas furnace that blasts hot air through the house with desert-storm efficiency, along with a living-room gas fireplace the designer built in as part of the guaranteed romance such a palace inspires. While I hack away at the onions, Stella opens a new bottle, gets the flames rising picturesquely. The living-room isn't shag, just a dark broadloom meant to hide the dirt. Like the bedrooms upstairs and the family-room, the ceiling is stucco—but since we're downstairs it's not pink but white. I wonder what it would be like to lie here, naked, in front of the romantic fireplace, looking up at the white stucco. Stella has already poured the wine. If the kids weren't here, I think to myself, we could try it right now. But of course the kids are here, because we tried it right now before, and so——. Etc., etc. Anyway, what kind of father am I, wanting my own children whom I don't really take care of to disappear so I can make more neglected children?

Stella now has on the kind of slacks women wear these days, wide hips, narrow little cuffs that hug their tiny ankles. One of those tiny ankles is crossed over her knee. She's sitting on one of the two matching white corduroy couches, reading a psychology textbook. That book, the master's degree program it's part of, was one of the reasons Stella gave for moving to town. It's basic to her plan, her master master's plan, at the end of which she'll have her own cube, not in a donut plaza off the highway but in a tastefully renovated downtown house, in which she'll "help women help themselves." She won't bother helping men help themselves, it goes without saying, because they already have, pigs at the trough, and if now they're sad and confused well, it's just like a kid who steals too many candies and then gets sick from eating too much. Or is disappointed because they stop tasting too sweet. Or angry that the people he robbed no longer like him.

While Stella reads her psychology text I dive into one of Carrie's magazines. It falls open to an article on composting vegetables. Almost every line is highlighted. I wish I could ask her how a person who lives in a house with stucco ceilings could spend her life composting vegetables but first of all she only lives in this house because she bought it to please Stella and secondly I've already asked her this kind of question and she doesn't even try to answer.

I switch to coffee so that by the time I'm laying the steaming plates of spaghetti out on the table, I'm stone sober. Stella, meanwhile, has flaked out on one of the white corduroy sofas. I find her lying on her back, one leg hooked over the back of the sofa, one hand flung out to the coffee table, still wrapped around her wine glass. Her cheeks are flushed, her face in unusual and angelic repose. Feeling like Santa Claus I rearrange her a bit and cover her with one of Carrie's fuzzy angora blankets.

During dinner I quiz the children about life in their new school. As if I am some interested relative who just dropped in from Mars, not the unstable father because of whom their mother had to move the children out of their natural home and into this same new school where they had to make all new friends and get used to different teachers.

Afterwards they show me their new room. Their pink stucco. They sleep in twin wood-framed beds that can be stacked to make bunks. On their beds are their favourite quilts, their stuffed toys, a few picture books I recognize. When I sit down on Crystal's bed she immediately snuggles up to me, demands that I read her a story about a brave worm, one I've read to her a thousand times before. Robbie pretends to be above all this. But he stretches out on his own bed and listens as I read.

One at a time I get them into their pyjamas, teeth and hair brushed, faces washed, the whole routine. Wind and snow are still rattling the windows. It is so warm here, so whole. I imagine the cabin, half-frozen and dark. As always, when I'm not there for the night, I feel uncomfortably disloyal, as if I've deserted my post.

When the children are ready I take them downstairs to kiss their mother goodnight. Stella is awake again, sipping a cup of coffee and reading in front of the fire. The children crowd around her. She draws them under the blanket. Soon they're chattering away, animated and oblivious.

That night we go to bed together as if I'd never left. So strange-familiar, Stella's body next to mine. This time when we make love it's like animals opening to each other in their cave. Stella falls asleep, holding me. When I wake up, she's still wrapped around my back. I listen to the snow and wind. There are nightlights in the hall and bathroom for the children, and when I close my eyes I can imagine those lights glowing outside, in the storm. My future self— or one of Stella's lovers—could be standing on the street, seeing the glow of these lights, speculating on the mystery behind the windows.

For hours I lie there, imagining myself being imagined. I am trying to believe I am really real, really here, really asleep in Stella's arms. But every time I close my eyes I float up above the house. First I see us, yes, the happy family happily ensconced in our gas-powered central-heated warmth. But then I go higher; the whole town is just a red-yellow smear of lights, and I am floating north, up the frozen ribbons of highway and then into the back country thick with scrub and beaver ponds. Until I come to the cabin, stranded and battered by snow, deserted by the only one who can love and watch over it.

5

In the morning I leave early, as the children are preparing for school. The snowploughs have passed in the night, my bucking Bronco has no problem blasting its way out of the driveway and into the street. I go to a restaurant for bacon and eggs, double brown toast no butter, a newspaper and endless coffee until my nerves set up a high whining chatter.

When I arrive at the office Frank looks up, then immediately starts talking the Redway deal we've been working on for months—a strip plaza location for which we levered the land, fought for all the clearances and permits, now are trying to unload in order to fill our bank accounts. Or at least pay our rent. Or something. It's so long since we've made a deal I can hardly remember the name of our lawyer.

This morning Frank is full of optimism. He's got on his lucky blue selling jacket, his face is shaved so close he looks like he's had his skin peeled. The blueprints are spread out on his desk and, this is how good Frank is, once he gets talking even I believe I can smell the fresh donuts and coffee from the little shop he's got marked out on the corner.

We're meeting the potential buyers in a downtown restaurant at noon, and just as we're getting ready to leave, Stella calls. Frank, giving me a big wink as if I'm about to pop the question, passes me the phone. I've just come out from our little washroom, my own face scraped raw by one of those disposable razors that you keep using for one more shave.

"How are you?" she asks.

"Nervous," I say. "We're trying to unload the plaza this morning."

Frank frowns. He doesn't like negative remarks except when he's into the nachos and beer.

"Good luck," Stella says, her voice empty. Of course she wasn't calling to ask about what I was or wasn't selling.

"I'll let you know how it goes later," I say, evading everything, leaving everything open. This is, as I often lecture my troops, known as taking possession of the high ground.

Stella responds with a direct and immediate attack. "Later?"

This is what it is to be Napoleon. This is what it is.

"I'll call you from the house," I concede, digging my own grave.

6

When I get home the snow is red with the setting sun. I go straight to the woodpile, letting my splitting axe say it all, its huge iron head rearing back in the darkness, then descending into the frozen wood with a loud mourning shriek.

Later that night I am out in the snow. The bucking Bronco is a dark outline in the moonlight, my own windows cast their golden glow like abandoned tears. As my skis scream softly on the frozen snow I am free to imagine that behind those gold-lit windows Napoleon is gathering his forces, charting out his marches, planning the conquests of new farflung empires, vast frozen hearts.

I move toward the pine woods. Thorns tear at my legs and face. Until finally I am safe in the darkness, dying to the shrill cries of winter owls, slivers of moonlight feasting on my blood.

Three Weeks

Libby Creelman

The three of them left Connecticut on the same morning, in a heatwave. Rosanna and Mike were subdued, already sweating. They waited as their mother turned the key in the front door lock, then as she stepped back and gave them one last look of worry and regret. She was wearing too much makeup and new clothes, carrying new suitcases. She told them she didn't want to say who she was going off with in case it didn't work out. Anyway, this time, it was no-one they knew.

"I'll call every day," she said, looking at Rosanna. "I promise. Then I'll see you both, right back here, in three weeks."

Mike couldn't help laughing. "Where did you think we were going, Mom?"

"I *know* where. The house in Maine."

"There's no phone there, Mom. Remember?" Rosanna sighed, hoping there was still a chance they might forget the whole thing. On either side of them their neighbours' sprinklers clicked round and round with that harmless tinny sound of summer.

Her mother lowered her suitcases and reached inside the collar of her blouse to rearrange something, briefly exposing her hard, straight collarbones. Then she kissed them both.

Inside her shorts' pocket Rosanna's fingers coiled around her last joint, so feather-light it seemed possible to lose it, even if it never left her pocket.

"Thanks, kids," her mother said gently. "Thanks for doing this."

Their cousin Peter met them in the trodden-down grass outside the kitchen door, bare-chested and grinning. He was as skinny at 24 as he had been at eight. He'd let his hair grow and it was pulled back now into a strangled ponytail on his bare back.

A shadow passed inside the old farmhouse, and a noise: something dropped or bumped into, then a murmured curse.

"How's the asparagus?" Mike asked.

Peter held a hand out waist high and announced, "Up to here on me already." He paused. "But I didn't know you were bringing a twelve-year-old."

"Sixteen, asshole," Rosanna said, but it was at this moment that a young woman appeared in the doorway behind Peter, who turned, his face bright, saying, "Haven't met Debbie, have you?"

She had short hair bundled in soft curls and a flawless face that seemed to carry with it a certain oblique vigour and influence. Rosanna could tell that Mike disliked her immediately, even before she used her stomach to prod open the screen door and emerge barefoot into the sunlight, her arms and legs covered in lilac speckles.

Peter placed his hand on her belly and said to Mike, "Three more months, Bud. Three more months and you're looking at Daddy."

"She's not fat, Mike. She's pregnant," Rosanna said as they darted up the field behind the house in order that Mike get his bearings after meeting Debbie and witnessing the change to the house. She was painting it purple. *Lilac.*

"That kitchen's going to be hard on my head," warned Mike.

"I saw some yellow paint too," Rosanna offered, wanting to pacify her brother, but also, to somehow elevate herself to his level of conversation.

"I can't wait for Louie to show."

Though this was the first Rosanna had heard of anyone named Louie, she said, "No kidding."

"Don't copycat," said Mike, who had always been fast. He reached over and popped his open hand across the back of her head so that her hair tossed into her eyes and she plunged into her next step. But it was a long shot from the old days.

When she lifted her head again they were just nearing the vegetable garden situated at the top of the field. Beyond the garden was a small grove of hardwoods, and beyond that, a second field. Rosanna hadn't been up there in years.

"If you say one word—one word, Rosanna—about what I have to tell you now, I'll go bananas. Do you read me?"

"Yeah."

"Positive?"

"Yeah!"

"You're staying in the house with Peter and *her*—"

"Since when?"

"Because there's only that one other bedroom and bla-bla-bla. And Louie, whenever he fucking gets his ass up here—"

"Where's he coming from?"

"His girlfriend. She's breaking up with him, basically. Anyway, my point is, Louie and I have been invited to stay in the bunkroom."

"How 'bout I stay in the bunkroom and you and Louie stay in the house?"

"Ha ha." A pause. "So we're clear on the sleeping arrangements?"

"Where's your plants? *The asparagus.*"

Mike gave her a fierce look, unsure of the extent to which he was being mimicked, and she moved a step away from him, her shoulders drawing inwards.

"You keep away from those plants, Rosanna. You're not in on it, do you read me?"

"So where do I do my shopping around here?"

"You gotta be the biggest pot-head I know. Sixteen fucking years old. Jesus fucking...."

She stopped abruptly in the path beside the pole beans and let him continue marching on, shaking his head. He halted after a few feet and turned back to look at her with a quizzical expression, as if she'd just asked him something. He was losing his train of thought.

She put her hand out. "That joint we smoked on the way up was my last."

"Already? You're out already?"

They gave up talking. Rosanna gazed back down at the farmhouse, which leaned to the west and was surrounded by a field intersected at odd angles by ragged stone walls. The house itself was a small cape with pitched roof and weathered, nearly white, clapboards. Black shutters had long fallen off and were stacked now in an attic corner, the paint lifting like the wings of dark moths. The house gave the impression, despite its recent history, of tidy domesticity and security. At the east end, attached to the small kitchen, was the woodshed—housing the bunkhouse, a 1970s addition—and attached to that, the gigantic barn. Both woodshed and barn were covered in rough shingles. There was no running water, electricity or telephone. The place had belonged to Rosanna's great-grandfather and then her grandmother on her father's side.

Peter and Debbie had been living in the house since June, when they put the plants in—both what Rosanna could see here in the garden, and whatever illegal bounty was now flourishing up in the other field. Rosanna had been hoping Mike might take her up there now, but it didn't look that way. For her, she realized, that field and those plants would be strictly off-limits.

It was hot. Insects were knocking themselves out in the corn and summer squash, zucchini and beets. There had been a lot of rain recently and every plant was green-swollen, luxurious under the blue sky, growing helter-skelter in all directions. The field swept out from beneath Rosanna's feet, then moved on down toward the farmhouse, circling round it before moving off to meet the dirt road. Heat waves were being cast up from the earth, engulfing the house, the woodshed and barn, Rosanna and Mike.

They had beets and zucchini for supper, and some dry corn-bread Peter had made, eating at the kitchen table beside the grubby-paned window. What Rosanna liked about this place was that in her lifetime, at least, there had never been a central female force maintaining it. It was always grimy, damp, cool, even in summer. The landscape outside might be basking with reproduction and heat, but here in the kitchen, where they were presently too stoned to say much, the temperature was ideal.

At last Peter looked at Mike and said, "Come on," and without another word they rose and left.

The kitchen door remained open, jammed on the flattened grass. Someone had detached the spring from the door frame, and Rosanna watched it swing from the open door. She lit another joint. Mike had given her a small supply, already rolled, which irked her. It was one of his many ways of exercising control over her. She liked to roll her own.

Debbie approached, smelling of oil paint. Her drum-tight stomach brushed Rosanna's shoulder. The thing she was wearing looked suspiciously like a nightie. It was hiked up in front on account of her stomach and if anyone had been interested, they could have easily seen what she wore as underwear.

It was careful work placing the joint between Debbie's fingers, since Debbie seemed to have trouble holding her hand steady. It was something Rosanna did reluctantly, anyway.

Then a shadow fell across the doorway and Debbie dropped the joint.

"Fuck fuck fuck," Debbie said, as she lowered herself without bending and began crawling beneath the table in search of the lit joint.

"Door was open," he said to Rosanna. "Sorry if I scared you." Then he glanced around the room. He was dark, not from the sun, but naturally, as if he'd been standing in the shadows of dense foliage too long and had grown to resemble his surroundings. When Rosanna saw the chunky class ring he wore, she experienced a sudden sinking; it seemed impossible to reconcile her friends and high-school life with what she was just beginning now with these strangers.

He asked her something, but she knew that the sound of her own voice might be a destructive thing. She needed to erase her existence from this kitchen.

As she passed through the low doorway and across the sloping floorboards, she considered her hair and clothes, the way she walked, aware that he was likely observing her. She headed for the sofa.

When she opened her eyes she was still high, still on the sofa. Her first thought was: *only moments have passed*, her second: *underneath these cushions there are my father's old Playboy magazines*.

Debbie was making room for herself beside Rosanna's legs, saying, "That happens to me sometimes." Then she produced a long, laboured sigh. "They went up back, Louie. Want me to show you?"

They were gone, and although it was what she had wished for, loneliness flooded Rosanna until she hurt, like she was only a rag dipped in a puddle of brown liquid so foul she'd wake tomorrow swollen.

She missed her mother. She missed home.

There was no television here, no pool, friends, malls. No

summer days of hanging out, doing nothing with girls she had known forever, girls with whom late at night, smoked up, a specific demented look or code word could bring on hysterical laughter. These people—her brother, a cousin, two strangers—were much older, in their twenties. It was frightening being with people you didn't know. They seemed to be a different species of animal. At any given moment you had no idea what thoughts they were having. You could wake in the middle of the night and have no knowledge of what they dreamed. Maybe you were in their dreams, but doing what?

Or they might be awake, you just wouldn't know. They might be touching one another.

Opposite the sofa was the fireplace and beside that, the brick oven, its cast-iron door marked, "Jacob Kimball, Portland, Me.", though Rosanna did not have to read this to know it was there. The door was slightly ajar, and Rosanna could see where inside the oven Debbie had placed her paint tins and brushes.

She rolled face-first into the back of the sofa. Its upholstery smelled of burning wood and old trunks. It smelled of the last century.

"You blacked out?" Mike was saying.

It was dark now in the house.

"Go away."

"Don't get stupid, Rosanna."

"Shut up. Go away."

He punched her shoulder. The sofa springs creaked beneath her and someone in the room inhaled sharply. "Rosanna, go to bed. We're gonna go look for a bar, all right, so just go to bed and don't smoke anymore or else."

"Maybe your sister wants to come," Louie suggested. Rosanna figured he was standing just inside the doorway; she couldn't see him where she lay.

"Or else what?" she asked.

30

"She's fucking sixteen, Louie. Look at her."

Rosanna woke the following morning bored, even before she stepped from her bed. She felt jailed. She felt overlooked. Mike had made it clear he didn't want her going anywhere near those plants. As if she were such a maniac she'd go up there and start tearing them all to shreds and stuffing them in her mouth.

The day passed, and then others, hushed and uneventful. Rosanna suspected that everyone was somewhere inside, either in the house or woodshed or barn, yet they remained hidden, as if involved with mysterious work forbidden to her. She knew there was nothing to caring for the plants at this point, unless watching them grow counted for something. It took her a while to realize that everyone was spending a lot of time asleep.

Not long into the morning, she would lock her doors and lie on her bed and light a joint. Her room was at the front of the house and had once been the parlour. The plaster walls were white, the wainscoting below muddy green. Fortunately, Debbie seemed uninterested in painting this room. The fireplace opposite Rosanna's bed was surrounded by modestly carved panelling, lending it a plain, dignified look that Rosanna found soothing.

If she rolled her head on the slab of blankets that served as her pillow, and gazed through light as white and calm as the inside of a blown eggshell, she could see her belongings dumped at the foot of the corner cabinet behind whose noble, ancient glass someone years ago had placed a collection of rocks and what were believed to be several arrowheads and chunks of petrified wood. Both the cabinet and simple fireplace opening Rosanna examined over and over as she lay, listening for sounds, for hours. The weight of her high kept her low, her spirits muffled. She felt tortured by a desire to surface, to search for something, yet at the same time felt safe in this room because there was nothing in

31

here to discover.

Once or twice a day she grew curious enough to venture out, though always avoiding Debbie who, without ever leaving the house, seemed to spend more time awake than anyone else as she travelled from bedroom to living-room to kitchen and back again with quick mincing steps that made her appear both officious and child-like.

Rosanna usually met Louie in the kitchen. She'd only be in there a minute, rooting for something in the cooler, when he'd come in through the woodshed entrance. He'd start talking to her and ask if she wanted to go for a walk and she would pretend she hadn't heard him and hurry back to her room. Once he even knocked on her door and spoke her name, but she ignored that too.

In the late afternoon she would wake from a nap she had never intended on taking, and hear voices again in the house. Groggy, she would turn to the window beside her bed and stare out at the hot humid air that met the landscape as if it would swallow it. The sky was blue-hazy with heat, yet there seemed no plant or insect that could suffer in this climate. Trees, saplings, grass, garden vegetables, thickets of vines, shrubs and wildflowers, all stood deceptively motionless, but growing nevertheless. Tricksters, vegetative reproduction: their growth was palpable. She knew that she was somehow witness to it, though powerless to see it with her eyes.

Sometimes at night a light rain fell and she would wake in her bed and picture it landing drop by drop on the narrow-fingered leaves of the plants up in the forbidden field blackened now by rain clouds. Pattering in ringlets on the soil surrounding each bulging stalk.

And then she would hear from within the house the creak of a voice or furniture, a sudden ping or muffled word, and she would turn onto her stomach and dig her head beneath the mildewed blankets.

32

At the end of each day, still a strong light in the sky after their meal of boiled vegetables and toast, they grouped in the cool, stale air of the living-room—originally the winter kitchen—and smoked up. Someone would suggest a trip to Shape's Lake to clean off, and Rosanna would wait, anxious to go, but in the end they only argued over when to begin harvesting, then staggered off to bed.

Rosanna sat on the raised hearth, a good distance from her brother, since his mood, as the days passed, grew increasingly jumpy. The ashes and clumps of charcoal in the hearth behind her gave off a sharp metallic aroma. The mineral remains of trees. The smell of wood ghosts, cold, sad. Growing and living that would never be again.

"I thought I heard a helicopter today," Mike said one evening. He flicked a piece of oatmeal cookie across the room. It landed neatly in Rosanna's hair.

"Fuck you, Mike," she said.

Peter was looking wearily at Mike. "They don't go over with helicopters anymore. I think I mentioned that to you about 81 times already."

At this, Debbie giggled, the sound of it a rutty laziness that Peter appeared unable to resist. He rose and began moving across the room toward her, taking, it seemed to Rosanna, hours. As if he were savouring the passage over, the anticipation.

Mike shifted with impatience, then shot several pieces of cookie at Rosanna.

"Look at the mess you're making," Louie said, annoyed. "You're a pig."

Peter arrived at Debbie's feet and lowered himself to his knees and took up one of her legs. She was wearing shorts, loose and negligible. He lifted the leg, straight as a broomstick, higher and higher, until it nearly touched her nose. It was clear to everyone that, pregnant or not, she had impressive flexibility.

When he released the leg it dropped like a log but he

caught it, a whisper above the floorboards. Then he picked up the other leg and began tossing both, one at a time, up and down like scissors. Debbie sat smiling remotely.

Mike rose. Louie was only a minute behind him. They were gone.

"Right here," Peter suggested after a while. He had Debbie's legs raised, but her knees were bent now, pinned wing-like on either side of her.

"I don't like that," Debbie said. She sounded winded.

He allowed her knees to drop slightly, no more than an inch. "Right here, Debbie. What do you say?"

Debbie looked across the room with mild curiosity. "We're not alone, stupid."

"Come on. Right here."

"Where'd your brother go?" Debbie asked Rosanna, who shrugged. "And that really gorgeous guy he's got with him?"

Peter sat back on his heels. "You mean the one with the ugly face?"

Debbie laughed generously, then spoke in a voice that drove Peter nuts. "He's gorgeous. Black hair, black eyes. If he was mine, I'd dress him in dark blues and marine greens. Every single day of his life." She tried to sit up but Peter immediately restrained her. She punched him twice on his shoulder, still teasing, still smiling. "What do you think, Rosanna? But I guess you're kinda young yet. Aren't you?"

Rosanna glanced at Debbie, reluctant to enter into a conversation with her. She turned her attention to her toes, spreading them over the floorboards and lifting her arches, pretending to be too preoccupied with her feet to have heard Debbie's question.

But Debbie was suddenly suspicious, her resentment of Rosanna descending out of the clear blue. "You *did* notice him. What a sneaky rat she is, Peter." She put her hands on Peter to push him off, but he was heavy and determined. She said again, "I don't like that."

Then she closed her eyes, forgetting Rosanna. Her head dropped forward with a languid nod. When Rosanna realized Peter's jeans were unbound, the waistline slipping down his white hips, she felt like an idiot, like a child.

Had the two of them dumped her by the side of a country road they could not have abandoned her more thoroughly than they did now. Rosanna swallowed and slipped her hands beneath her thighs. Her palms were cold where they lay over the gritty bricks, the tops of her hands warm where they met her own skin. Her mother would want her to leave the room immediately. Even Mike would want that.

Several mornings later Mike, Louie and Peter headed up to the second field with uneasy agreement and two chainsaws between them. Rosanna watched from inside the farmhouse until they had disappeared through the stand of trees separating the two fields.

"This constant scared shitless business," Debbie said, slumped on the sofa. "It'll end once they get the harvest in." She pushed herself upwards and her voice grew stronger. "Businessmen, man, I tell ya. They think they're soooo important. Soooo grown-up. Bringing in the bacon. They crack me up."

For over an hour they listened to the distant whine of the chainsaws. Then Debbie put together a picnic lunch and invited Rosanna to help her carry it.

Mike looked up as they approached and Rosanna saw the crippling fear cross his face before he recognized them. He was that wound up. Instinctively, she kept away from him. The field had originally been used for grazing cattle—too hilly for cultivation—and was now nearly disguised by the invasion of small spruce and pine. But Rosanna, curious and relieved to be here at last, cast her eyes over the landscape and easily picked out the plants: that unmistakable nutty shade of green, so plainly non-native, uniform in height, and mostly bud, which she knew, of course, was good.

Half lay fallen, already cut. Louie was dragging them off the field into a dark feathery heap in the shade.

Along one edge of the field ranks of steeplebush and meadowsweet were blooming and here Debbie threw out the blanket she'd taken from the bed she and Peter shared. She set out the fluffernutter sandwiches, popcorn, cold water, hot boiled vegetables. Then she sat and waited.

"Didn't we just have breakfast?" Peter complained, flopping down on the blanket and picking up a sandwich.

"Oh, Louie," Debbie called out in a voice sing-song, motherly, strained. "Oh, Mike."

"Take a break, guys," Peter said. Then, "Are ya deaf?"

The mood was tense. Rosanna figured it had been tense all morning. She wondered if they'd notice if she rose now and went off back down to the house. Yes, they would. Peter had felt the plants could go another week, easily. Mike and Louie thought the time was now. Why wait for disaster. For hammering rain. For helicopters moving over the countryside like gigantic roving eyes.

Debbie suddenly glanced at Rosanna with a look both beseeching and confiding. As if they were pals. But what could Rosanna do? How could she entice Mike and Louie to come take up a sandwich and express gratitude to Debbie?

At last Debbie rose to her feet in several distinct stages and went into the hot field, her quick short steps ill-fitting outside the dark farmhouse. Both Rosanna and Peter strained to hear her words as she leaned over Mike, then Louie, her hand on the lower centre of his drenched back. Rosanna watched the three straggle toward her. She noticed how soft and droopy their clothes had grown through lack of washing, yet the memory of each person's individual body shape seemed present in their clothing. The effect was personal, intimate. Rosanna realized her own clothes would look that way, too.

Neither Louie nor Mike seemed inclined to share the

blanket but sat just beyond it. After several minutes Mike grew comfortable in the shade. White fluff ringed his lips. When Rosanna crossed behind him he spun suddenly on his rear and whipped a leg into her path. He grinned as she went over, spilling her water on the blanket. The steamy scent of wet dirty cloth rose into the air.

And then he couldn't stop harassing her, like a puppy driven to tearing furniture or ankles. He tripped her, shoved her, tossed and rubbed food into her face and hair, down the neck of her shirt.

Rosanna waited it out, knowing that any attempt to escape would be a mistake. She sat cross-legged, head bowed, until Mike had flicked the last of his vegetables onto her lap.

In the silence she heard a bluejay and looked up. Except for Mike, they were all watching her. Peter looked mesmerized; Louie either curious or amused; and Debbie so jolly her face nearly rippled with it. A flood of hate for them swept through Rosanna. In her mind's eye she watched herself closing the distance between herself and Debbie, ripping out great gobs of her hair, tearing those delicate cheeks, kicking that belly. Hurting her in such a way that Mike's actions would be utterly eclipsed.

But she got dizzy when she stood quickly and that forced her to wait and by then she'd lost her courage. She turned to go, accepting that Mike could make her short passage across the field to those trees a miserable hell.

Bodies shifted behind her, footsteps pounded, there was a rush of movement, a grunt, a thud. Rosanna walked on, waiting for Mike to tackle her. When he didn't, she glanced back to find Louie and Mike rolling in the dry grass with such a yearning to destroy each other they might have been reading her thoughts. They might have leapt from her mind. As if she might reclaim her feelings and return them to their secret place, she took a step toward them, then stopped, her hands at her sides. Slowly, she gave those feelings up. She let Mike and Louie keep them.

She gazed at the hazy liquid sky, the evergreens ringing the field, at Debbie and Peter posed like dolls in a pile of toy plates and cups and one filthy blanket. Where her heart should have been there was an object the size of a plum or hard-boiled egg. It had always interfered with her breathing and eating.

The energy with which Mike and Louie first went at each other began to slacken. There was a rush of wrestling movement, an abrupt ugly pause as Louie pinned and held Mike, then another rush, a rearranging of limbs and suddenly Rosanna remembered Debbie's knees pinned away from her body and Peter as he knelt quickening against her: once started, nothing could have stopped him. She saw them screwing in their bed, in the woods, on that blanket. And somehow, each time, Rosanna was responsible.

Louie shook Mike, though Mike lay surrendered on his back on the ground, then rose over him and shouted, "You're a pig." He was panting, his hair bunched over his forehead. "If I had a sister I would like her. I would take care of her. You're disgusting. You know that?"

They searched for Rosanna for hours, or at least Louie, Debbie and Peter searched for her, called for her, walked right by her. When Mike found her, after dark, it was only because he chose to. She was hiding where she had always hidden. He crawled up into the small space over the roof of the inside privy at the back of the barn where she crouched, hidden by rolls of chicken wire, a stack of metal buckets and very little light.

"Anyone had a dump recently?" he joked.

"No, but Debbie has had a number of pisses. Talked to herself, too, but I couldn't hear what. Something about Peter."

He looked at her. Her face was dusty and had that moist look that couldn't have been just from sweat. She'd been crying. He took care of her, didn't he? Of course he did. Shit, looked like Louie wanted the job though. The thought softened him to Louie. And to Rosanna.

He helped her down, then the two of them returned to the kitchen where Mike sat at the kitchen table looking out at the first stars while Rosanna made a jam sandwich. He wanted to say something to her, but what? He tried to imagine what their mother might say. The way she might at this moment console Rosanna.

When Debbie started through the doorway he snarled, and she turned back, looking indignant and crushed. He didn't want anyone coming near Rosanna tonight.

They tied the plants up in the barn. Mike invited Rosanna to help and stood by her, at least the first day, showing her how to strip the greasy, rose-coloured buds and discard the curled leaves, reminding her over and over not to touch her eyes with her hands. At best, from a distance—outdoors or in the house—the smell was sweet, like cloves, like Christmas cookies, honeyed and luscious. She lay in her bed at night and it lingered in the air above her as a reminder of her day, standing across from Louie, his class ring flashing in the gloomy light as he stripped buds as thick as his thumb.

Inside the barn, the doors closed and everyone silent, the smell was more pungent, rank, skunk-like. Even Peter seemed uneasy. Rosanna watched each time as Debbie, though she should have known better, put a finger into an eye and moments later—the door banging open, Peter cursing—went reeling outside where she stood gagging not far from the house.

But even this, Rosanna liked. The close, overwhelming odour, the illicit risk. The possessing of these forbidden plants and all that the soil and sun and rain had given them.

39

The second day they quit early, weak and careless from one head rush after another, the sticky organic dust having found its way into every crack of skin and clothing.

They were the only people at Shape's Lake and swam naked. Peter moved slowly nearer Debbie in a silent game of his own that the rest tried to ignore.

Rosanna avoided everyone, submerging and opening her eyes, forcing her mind to narrow on a single pin-point of thought: let the others drown and disappear. Disappear, disappear, she began to chant aloud, forgetting she was underwater, so that bubbles came out of her mouth and went rushing to the surface like round, explicit signals.

She waited until everyone was out, then hurried to shore into the circle of pine trees where she had undressed, stepping over needles perfumed and spongy. A squirrel hidden from view began to natter on at her: fearful, annoyed, curious. A woodpecker hammered bark with a momentum and beat that suggested he'd not taken a rest in years. A pinched shriek from Debbie shot past and was gone. Rosanna heard all this with a precision that touched her, though she did not know it.

She had her shirt on and was balancing on one foot, poised to step into her underpants, when she heard footsteps and realized suddenly several things: she was half dressed and wet, her clothes were dirty, she would be starting Grade 11 in only a week.

Louie was passing, on his way to the road.

She stepped quickly into her underpants and began yanking them up. Pine needles on the soles of her feet dropped into the crotch. She knew that Louie had stopped, that he could not resist noticing this. She swiped at the needles, gave up and pulled at her underpants but they rolled under and tangled on her wet thighs.

"Wait. Don't," he said, coming over. He leaned down and lifted the crotch at the sides and shook it until it was cleared of debris. Then he moved his fingers around one of her thighs, then the other, thoughtfully and with his face averted like a person picking a raffle ticket from a hat, and untangled her underwear. Despite some distant, dreary mortification, she waited to see if he would pull them up.

As the squirrel rounded a trunk only a few feet away, its voice gone, its tail swishing, its need to see getting the better of it, she stared at Louie's head bent over her, at the tight curls of black hair flashing with oil and water. Here was a proximity to something she had not planned on. He was a man. And he was very near. I'm only sixteen, she wanted to remind him.

She thought he would say, "What are you afraid of?" because that's what boys had said before, but he said nothing.

It was only when she realized her underpants were stained an ugly yellow that she blushed. Louie straightened with an expression she could not read. As he walked off across the needle floor she considered how remarkable it was that his breath should have felt so hot.

When she reached the road they were all there, waiting for her, reluctant to get back into the stuffy car; instead, roaming over the road which had only recently been paved. Fresh, oily chunks of tar were crumbling into gutters already caked with pine needles, leaves, twigs, slippery amphibians. When no-one would meet Rosanna's eye, she knew they had been witness to Louie helping her with her underwear in the pine woods clearing.

Peter got in behind the wheel and Debbie slid in beside him. Louie took the back and left the door open for Rosanna, who put her hand on the sun-scorched handle without feeling it.

Mike hesitated before getting in the front. After a while he began rolling down his window. "Too much?" he asked, turning slowly, reluctant to make eye contact with his sister.

The wind was lifting Rosanna's wet hair and drying the curled tips. She said, no, not too much. She liked it, in fact.

She watched the countryside pass by, her thoughts drifting to her mother—they would all be home soon and she was glad. Her face was turned instinctively away from the other passengers. But something about the look of the trees against the distant no-colour sky gradually made her impatient. When she finally thought about Louie, she realized it would be a long courtship.

The Hidden Life of Doges

(EXCERPTS FROM THE FIRST KNOCKOFF OF ELIZABETH
MARSHALL THOMAS'S SURPRISE BEST-SELLER)

Bruce McCall

There is an air of mystery about doges that all too easily slides into superstition, the most notorious being that doges instinctively seek only power to control the coffers and courts of Venice and Genoa. Also, that they are happiest sitting in great drafty stone rooms writing indecipherable edicts. That they speak Latin because they have to, not because they choose to. That when one doge meets another, he reflexively begins to plot the other's downfall, but never acts overtly to that end.

Three doges boarded at my suburban home for several years. Salvatore, the pint-size but endearing one, forever begging for yet another cannoli, was left by a friend. Enrico and Luigi—having evidently sensed Salvatore's presence with their big, uncanny Adriatic noses—simply camped on the doorstep until admitted to the household. Enrico was imperious and magisterial, the alpha doge. Luigi, the plump, bumbling, comic doge, forever spoiling his beautiful parchment pronunciamentos with drool, was altogether a card, yet terrified of gondolas and reduced to mewling despondency by the sound of lute music.

To my astonishment, almost nothing about the everyday lives of doges had been written since they first appeared, in the Middle Ages. Scardini's *It's a Doge's Life*, widely considered the standard text, was deeply superficial ("...your average doge likes wearing funny hats; nobody knows why"), while *The Great Picture Book of Doges* was just that and only that, lacking even captions. No-one had ever shadowed a doge or watched him take a bath or anything. Nowhere to be found was any hint of an answer to the most basic questions: What makes doges tick? Beneath their impassive demeanours, behind their arcane rituals—what do doges really want?

Having nothing better to do, I decided to observe my small gaggle, up close and personal: follow them around, read their mail, go through their stuff when they were out of the house—and perhaps, by and by, develop a set of sweeping generalizations about the hidden life of doges.

Salvatore hated Enrico—or so it initially seemed. He would lift his chin and sniff regally whenever Enrico barked out another of his new edicts. But after closely watching the two interact, I found that the real purpose of Salvatore's haughty disdain was to lure Enrico into an intellectual duel. His lips would move as Enrico spoke; he was repeating and memorizing every word, while feigning lack of interest. His shaggy head would nod up and down, despite himself, or shake vigorously from side to side, indicating disagreement and disapproval. Clearly, the two were engaged in the ancient doge rite of mutually sharpening their intellectual skills, for it was on the suppleness and subtlety of their brainpower that the doges' position in society, and often their very survival, always depended.

Luigi, meanwhile, would become hopelessly lost and confused in articulating even the simplest plan or idea. He would begin to speak and then immediately start circling back to where he'd begun, throwing Salvatore and Enrico into frenzies of frustrated yapping as they tried to follow him. But this was far from being the sign of mental indiscipline that it seemed: Luigi was performing the doges' instinctive act of bamboozling the competition, honed over countless decades of the political infighting for which they had been bred.

44

Soon enough, indeed, Salvatore and Enrico themselves would start off a conversation and then lose their way, repeating the same obvious points, omitting nouns and verbs, haring off on wild-goose chases about the weather or naval provisions. By bedtime, all three would be left spent, and panting with exhaustion. But the very next morning they would be at it again. This elaborate and seemingly pointless skirmishing was for them a meaningful and necessary form of gamesmanship, doge-style.

I noticed that the comfort-loving doges all tended to be in a constant state of itchiness, rubbing their necks and chests and armpits vigorously but to no apparent effect. Yet the salves and powders I offered always met silent rejection, inevitably accompanied by an expression that as much as snarled, "You crazy?" It seemed a cruel and bewildering affliction, until one day I realized that the cause was the very clothing they wore—coarse brocades and furry capes and collars—and that these garments were the doges' outward sign of rank. Far from being an affliction, all that itching and writhing was, in the doges' world, a precious symbol of high status.

Enrico, the eldest doge, would always take the big BarcaLounger in the corner while the other two meekly sat in attendance on the sofa. If Enrico happened to be upstairs napping, or off at the mall again shopping for quill pens, Salvatore or Luigi would make a beeline for the BarcaLounger. On Enrico's return, there would be no confrontation; the temporary BarcaLounger occupant would slink away, back to the sofa. Just as their forebears had done centuries ago in Venice and Genoa, these doges practiced a self-regulating way of avoiding open conflict—obviously a survival tactic designed to prevent enemies from threatening their power by driving a wedge between them.

One by one, under close observation, the doge myths toppled. Doges do see in colour: Enrico ordered *Viva Las Vegas* from Blockbuster Video twice as often as he ordered

The Cranes Are Flying. A doge *will* eat fruits and vegetables—but only fresh; as if he were ruled by some primitive, pre-Birds Eye *Ur-hunger*.

Do doges have a sense of humour? No, if folklore is to be believed. And yet Enrico would spontaneously turn on the TV to watch reruns of *Gilligan's Island* and sit there snickering, his teeth showing in a curious, rictus-like grin. Salvatore, for his part, liked to play 52 Pickup with Luigi and would whoop with delight as the deck of cards fluttered all over the parlour and a long-faced Luigi, suckered once more, stooped to pick them up.

According to received wisdom, doges take walks to go to church, to inspect the Navy and to visit the Council of Ten for a game of backgammon. I determined to verify this by following the trio on Friday evenings, when Enrico arose from his BarcaLounger, yawned, and announced that he and his companions were "going out to stretch our legs."

It was ever the same: Enrico, Salvatore and Luigi, walking three abreast, followed the same route into town—down Maple Street, left at Main, then a right at Jefferson. In midblock they would stop and, after lightly grooming one another, slip into P. J. Monahan's at the precise moment happy hour began.

What inborn sense of timing told them it was happy hour (for all three eschewed wristwatches) is one of those ineffable mysteries of the doge. Two hours later, at exactly 7 PM, when happy hour ended, they would emerge, swatting one another with their ducal bonnets, jumping over fire hydrants, singing a kind of pre-Renaissance doo-wop: tension-relieving doge play, as old as Venice and Genoa themselves. Then they would boisterously lope down Jefferson, lurching and weaving now, yet by some deep instinct repeating the same complex movements every time: into the Topless Lounge for fifteen minutes, then next door to the Adult Videomat, across the street to the Blimpie Base, back to the Topless Lounge, diagonally over to All-Nite

Billiards; then, at last, slowly and uncertainly and always just when the cock crowed, retracing their steps back home —touchingly making certain to scrape their feet on the sisal doormat before going in.

Enrico met an Italian bar girl and moved in with her. Once regular, their Sunday-afternoon visits tailed off and then ceased altogether. Luigi, on his way home early one Saturday, wandered into the street and was hit by a bus. My friend came back one day soon afterward to retrieve Salvatore, who had taken to spending his lonely days curled up in the BarcaLounger, watching MacNeil/Lehrer and sending out for pizza. They left that night for Cincinnati; from the way Salvatore rushed to the door and clambered into the car without so much as a backward glance, I knew that he knew, in his inscrutable doge way, that it was time to go.

Goombay Smash

Jane Eaton Hamilton

The hotel was what your travel agent, a gay man who gave you an itinerary with a sixteen-hour layover in Toronto, recommended. He showed you an advertisement in *Girlfriends* magazine. Two women sunning in *chaise-longues* were photographed from the rear; only two tanned, fit arms showed and then, beyond them, the swimming-pool, and then, beyond that, some potted palms. It looked like paradise and you were keen to sign up. Now that you're actually here, you know that as far as décor goes, the resort is passably nice, although the pool is teacup-sized. There's a jacuzzi, with palm trees skittering in the breezes. Your room is undeniably cramped, with hardly enough space for all your and Marg's luggage, which in very short order opens like orifices and ejaculates vibrators and sandals and haemorrhoid cream. In the window the apparently broken air-conditioner burbles; the room is as cold as a refrigerator. You spend your first night in the defrost drawer, huddling against Marg like a stick of celery. The good part is that, tossed together under the covers, you and she make love, and if there's a little something missing after five years together, at least she's having sex with you, not someone else.

Although the room was billed as "poolside," it does not escape your attention that the puddle they call a pool is down a long hall, through a courtyard and then through the dining-room into a second courtyard. Nor has it gone

48

unnoticed that no-one could swim in it, not really, that it's too tiny for more than a single crawl stroke end to end.

The morning stretches out leisurely. There is a breakfast of sorts served in the dining-room, with coffee, orange juice, toast and cereal. As promised in the glossy brochure, there are plenty of women. Only women, in fact, and they mostly come in twos, like Ark animals. You and Marg take your plates to the courtyard and sit in partial shade at a white resin table. "Heh, Marg," you say and when she looks up at you, you send her the visual equivalent of an elbow in her side. You want her to look at all the sets of twins. For instance, the two women who wear the same white serge baseball shirts, with black trim that says "Key West" as if it's a team. The women are young, probably in their mid-twenties. You can't for the life of you imagine what they do when they aren't busy with a tropical vacation: are they accountants? Historians? This hotel doesn't come cheap. They have identical blond hair, spiky on top but roping between their shoulder-blades in back. Are they perhaps actual twins? No, they smooch. They look longingly across their table at each other and rise to plant wet kisses on each other's lips.

It would be like kissing yourself, you think, and think about how many nights you've been left to do just that.

There is another couple who wear their identically styled hair blown pouffily back. One is streaked blond and the other is brunette, but that's not what you notice. What you notice is the sameness, and their similar thin lips. When they depart, going off to do you don't know what with their day in paradise, another couple takes their spot. Though different in build, both of these women have masses of curly black hair cascading to their waists.

Maybe this is how American lesbians celebrate their anniversaries, you think. Never mind paper, silver, gold: American lesbians have hair anniversaries. If they make it

49

two years, they part on the same side, five years they spike, ten and they bob. Twenty and they both wear buns in snoods.

"Psst," you say, "Marg. Look over there."

Marg says, "What, Joyce?" and looks up at you.

You point out the women with waterfall hair and try and explain about hair anniversaries, and how the two of you should get matching buzz cuts, but Marg just frowns and goes back to scraping out her grapefruit with a stumpy handled spoon.

You hope if you live to be 90, you never look like anyone's clone. Unless it's Marg's. You would be Marg's clone if she asked. You would—if she asked.

You rented a car in Miami. When you called your mother to say you were a bit hesitant about renting at the airport, she said, "Don't be silly. They only kill Germans." You drove down the southern seaboard through the linked group of southern Florida islands called the Keys. Because it is late October, every home or business you passed, just about, was decorated. Americans take their Hallowe'en seriously. In Vancouver, where you live, Hallowe'en is reserved for the few days immediately preceding the end of the month: a simply carved pumpkin on the doorstep, a demure bowl of candy in the foyer. But in Florida porches are massed in white cotton pulled out to resemble spider webs. These are huge, ten or twenty feet across. Black plastic spiders galumph across the netting. In every second window, convincing fright masks made of rubber are displayed along with white-sheeted ghosts or black-sheeted witches. Maybe it's the tropics. Everything here is ripe and half rotten, even holidays.

Ways you have debased yourself for her:

1) you have lain nude on your car, a gigantic hood ornament, in your garage that smells of dirty oil, waiting for her

to raise the door with her remote;

2) you have danced naked to girl-group songs in your kitchen;

3) you have served her chocolate birthday cake in your birthday suit, coming to her with your breasts illuminated by candlelight.

There is something disorienting about breakfast. For one thing, you are smack dab in the middle of a bunch of vacationing lesbians, which means you ought to feel like a hog in heaven. But you don't. Instead you feel pasty-skinned and overweight, as if you carry the heaviness of Canada with you. No-one looks at you. No-one cruises you. You might as well be a table. Or a pumpkin.

Vines hang down the sides of the buildings trailing things that look to you like red licorice ropes. Hibiscus shrubs bloom hot and pink, thrusting up deeply coloured stamens. Everything droops and drips. Oranges plump on leafy stems, changing from green to orange. The hot tub gurgles. Although you wish it weren't true, skeletons dangle from some of the palm trees. When you were thinking about taking Marg away somewhere, you researched palm trees and found out there were 3000 varieties. There are probably ten or twenty varieties around the courtyard. You try to dredge up names: coconut, saw cabbage, Royal.

You are almost positive Marg doesn't want to be here with you. She's made it clear. When you said, *Let's get away,* she said, *What? You and me?*

While Marg finishes eating, you go to the office to ask for a room upgrade. You want a suite right beside the pool because, as you tell Camille, you didn't come thousands of miles to stay in a room the size of a closet. "I gave closets up years ago," you say, grinning. Camille doesn't think it's funny. There is a room you can change to at noon, she says, for an extra $30 US a night; if you pack, Camille will see that your bags are moved. Even if you get back late, someone will be in the office to exchange keys with you. Camille is a strapping blond who wears a white shirt calculated to set off her dark tan. As far as you can see, there is only one of her. She asks if you and Marg have signed up for tomorrow's women-only sunset champagne cruise. You say, "Should we?" as if Camille will know what's the right move to please Marg, then plunk $80 US, which works out to something like $8000 Canadian, on her desk and wait for a receipt.

Marg and you stroll out to discover Key West. You walk to where a marker tells you you're at the southernmost tip of the continental US. Cuba, it says, is only 90 miles away. You think of the refugees trying to cover the distance by raft; you shake the thought, a responsible, work-a-day concern, away and try to concentrate on paradise. Walk to the water's edge. Point at your chest. Say, "These are the southernmost boobs in the continental US."

Marg laughs, which you consider such a hopeful sign that you mention hair anniversaries again.

You watch pelicans dive-bomb for food. You love their greedy pouches and how they skim the surface of the waves looking for fish. Florida birds astonish you. In a restaurant parking-lot on the way down, you and Marg saw a flock of tall, red-legged white birds that you believe were ibis. And you've noticed a white heron, too, standing in the ocean shallows by the side of the highway.

It's hot out so every store becomes a relief, both from the heat and the street vendors who promise the cheapest T-shirts in America. There's merchandise for sale that you'd never find in Vancouver, and lots of art galleries; while Marg leans on the doorframe, assuredly bored, you buy three framed prints and arrange to have them shipped home.

On Duval Street, you buy a black ostrich feather, look hard at Marg and say, *For later*.

Marg wants to tour the Hemingway House. Hemingway was never a favourite writer of yours but because Marg's happiness is paramount and because old houses fascinate you, you agree. Also, you see it as a chance to get off your feet, if only for a minute. Key West is supposedly a walker's paradise, but you can attest first hand that touring has hardly been like walking on clouds. Asphalt is asphalt and after a while, the balls of your feet ache no matter how pretty the scenery. And there's been some pretty good scenery. Especially the flora, the wild, untamable growth that loops and spirals through people's yards messy as intestines.

There is a little while before a tour begins so you and Marg wait, examining a brochure, sitting on the lip of a mosaic-tile fountain in the courtyard. The house is a registered historic landmark. It's big and blocky, painted beige, with wonderful oval windows with green shutters, a Spanish Colonial made with local brick. The grounds are perfect; philodendrons mass and climb banana palms, dangling leaves as big as boogie boards.

And in fact the tour is lovely, too—the house is warm and sweet. You long to reach out and run your fingers across the spines of the books in the many bookshelves, even though you know most of the books were probably not Hemingway's. But many of the furnishings are genuine, things Hemingway and his wife Pauline accumulated in Spain, Africa and Cuba. There's a wonderful birthing chair in the master bedroom that belonged to Pauline; Pauline had two kids with Ernest and you wonder if she used the chair. A sign strapped across it says, "Please do not sit in this chair." You wonder about being a scofflaw and sitting anyhow. You wonder what you would give birth to.

Hemingway built the first pool in Key West. It is filled and blue and beautiful, much nicer than the chary one at the guesthouse where you're staying. Apparently it about broke Hemingway—even in the late thirties, the cost was

$20,000. That's why he sunk a penny—his last, according to legend—in the wet cement of the patio.

Marg says her favourite thing is the catwalk from his second-storey bedroom to his office over the poolhouse.

"Aren't writers romantic?" she asks dreamily. She taps the brochure on your arm. "It says he wrote *A Farewell to Arms* and *For Whom the Bell Tolls* here."

Marg once booked you into the Sylvia Beach Hotel in Newport, Oregon. The only room left was the Hemingway Room, which had a view of the parking-lot and an even better view of the Dempsy Dumpster. Worse, it had a moth-bitten deer head right above the bed. You dreamed that it fell and one of its antlers gored you though your heart.

One of the many, six-toed cats slinks around your ankles, its malformed paws flattening on the porch boards. The air smells like jasmine.

Mallory Pier: it's where you end up after a long afternoon of walking, staring the sun in its swollen orange eye as it winks into the Caribbean. Night falls, but all around you are hucksters. An acrobat totters across a wire strung fifteen feet above the boardwalk. A sword swallower pushes blades that look black and deadly into his throat. A boy of about fifteen grins while tourists take snaps of the iguana on his shoulder. A bearded men lets his parrot hop on tourists' shoulders then asks for donations. It's busy. It's noisy. It's colourful. It mirrors your mood. All that cacophony, that jostling, that competition for your attention. That's what it's like inside you. There isn't a calm neuron in your entire brain. They're all roused. They're all snapping and popping to the Latin music of the pier. You could burst into dance any second, something as disjointed and arrhythmic as a wooden puppet.

You're almost positive that she gives the other woman

things you've given her.
Where is your watch?
My watch?
The watch I gave you for Christmas.

Where is that ear cuff I gave you?
Ear cuff? I don't know. Did you give me an ear cuff?

This has been going on for months. Something has been going on for months. That's why you're here, why you planned this trip—to have Marg all to yourself, to have her undivided attention. At home, Marg is a very busy chef in a very busy restaurant and, as far as you can tell, also a very busy lover—although not in your bedroom.

At home, you have taken to watching the Discovery Channel while you wait up for Marg. Recently, they had a week's special on sharks. Sharks, researchers contend, are as intriguing as whales and dolphins. But after watching eight specials, you don't agree. You don't see anything interesting about sharks. Not great whites, not whale sharks, not hammerheads. They don't vocalize. They don't breach. They don't even breathe air. They're fish, not mammals, and that's what the researchers seemed to forget. The only thing that intrigued you, especially considering the upcoming trip to Key West, was an aerial shot of a man and a woman standing in water just thigh high. Dotted around them, each within 50 yards, were seven great white sharks. According to the TV, the ocean is like that all the time; the announcer offers up the image to prove that sharks only rarely attack humans. They would only like you kicking on a surfboard so that, from underneath, in their stupid, subterranean brains, you looked like a sea lion. You and Marg together—twin sea lions.

You and Marg recently bought a house together. Naively, you assumed this meant that the two of you were seriously committed. Because as a teacher you have summers off, you started to putty and scrape, mostly alone, in July. In early August, when you moved your bed to start painting the walls in there, a note fluttered to the floor from under Marg's pillow: *What am I doing?* it asked. *She's young enough to be my daughter.*

Although you are not personally that young, you know who is. Her name is Emma. She's the new sous-chef at Marg's restaurant. She is young, skinny and married. She wears a lot of black.

When you get back to the guesthouse, your belongings have appeared miraculously in the "suite" beside the pool. At this guesthouse, where the rooms are the size of closets, the suites are the size of rooms. They are only called suites because that sounds good in the brochure. Some women are having a party outside; you and Marg decide to try the jacuzzi, which is abandoned. But as it turns out, someone has sprinkled soap into it and when you turn on the jets, it begins to foam. At first it is hard to see the bubbles; in the dark night they make only the ghostliest, Hallowe'en outline, but after a while, the bubbles begin to pop against the bottom of your chins, against your lower lips, against your noses. When Marg inhales one she giggles and says, "I think we should call it a night." You swat bubbles away, cupping them like breasts. You step from the tub, which spills suds, and pull towels around yourselves. You tiptoe through the breakfast room You half hope the partying women will ask you to join them. You wonder if there is something identifiably Canadian about you. Perhaps your pasty skin reminds them of snow. Perhaps they understand that you are the kind of woman upon whom your lover would cheat.

You crawl into bed beside Marg. You want to be held in her arms, but she has her shin in her hand. She is dotting After Bite where the mosquitoes have got her. Into her leg she says, "First there was nothing, and then there was *A*

Farewell to Arms. I'm still trying to get over it."

The women outside hoot and holler. You think of a man who lives across the street from you in Vancouver. Occasionally you see him with his hose in the street, kneeling, hosing the litter that has accumulated away from the front of his yard. Some goes left. Some goes right. He keeps checking to make sure his neighbours aren't watching him.

You wonder who has stayed in this bed before you, whether they number in the dozens or hundreds, whether they've left pieces of themselves behind in the form of stray hairs or dandruff or stains, whether they were new lovers or old, whether any of them fought. You are not fighting with Marg, of course, and that has to count for something. It is not exactly a honeymoon between you, but not fighting has to count for something. You think about Key West's narrow streets, the small saltbox houses, their gingerbread trim. You walked past a small store with half of its wares on its outside wall. A woman in a yellow dress tended it.

"May I take a picture?" Marg asked and the woman, cackling, waved her hand.

You blinked at each other, trying to decide if that meant yes or no. The hands of an antique clock circled too quickly. A sign said, "Thank you, EMORY." There was a lifesize baking mould of C3PO from *Star Wars*. There was a bunch of plastic bananas, a trombone, a washboard, a coconut monkey's head and a sign with a Fitzgerald-like character in tennis whites under the word "Goombay."

You lie in bed listening to the party from which you are excluded. Marg puts down her After Bite and sighs. "I wish to hell they'd just shut up," she says, and as if in answer, you hear an interruption. Marg slides from bed and reports from the window. "It's the police," she whispers. "They've had a complaint. They're breaking it up."

It is after one when you finally slide into sleep.

You wake groggy, as if you were one of the drunks at the party. The sun bakes at the window. Marg is nowhere to be found. You stumble to the bathroom and remember that today is the day the guesthouse moves you back to your old room with the broken air conditioner. This room is booked. This is also the day of the sunset champagne cruise. Tomorrow, leaving Key West, you will visit an alligator swamp before heading to the airport. Maybe Marg is at breakfast. Yes, yes, she is. When you join her, slipping into a moulded booth in the breakfast room, you're aware that people are finally noticing you. But they don't seem very friendly. The twins in the Key West baseball jerseys actually shoot you the finger. Marg shrugs. She says, "They think we're the ones who reported them."

You wonder if Marg is missing Emma; if she came to breakfast alone because she couldn't stand to be near you another minute. You remember that once upon a time, things were new and fresh between the two of you. Marg's eyes danced the Macarena when you came into a room. You aren't hungry. You brave the shattering glances and serve yourself a small bowl of unflavoured yogurt. It's sour. It puckers your lips.

After thumbing through tourist brochures, Marg has an idea for the day. She wants to rent scooters.

"Scooters? As in motorcycles?" Perhaps you screech, because three sets of twins turn to give you scathing glances. Has Marg seen how Key West drivers drive? Maybe she wants you to die. Maybe she wants the insurance money so that she can open a restaurant with Emma. If you're lucky, you'll end up a vegetable and Marg will have to nurse you the rest of your natural born days. "I can't ride a motorcycle."

"See?" Marg says and passes you a brochure. She taps it. "They give you lessons on the spot."

That is how the two of you end up scorching through Old Town like Hallowe'en rockets. The scooters aren't so hard to manage, after all, but you'd prefer to stick to the back roads, where it doesn't matter if you give it too much gas and fly. Marg has an idea. You scooter out through a military base to a public beach. Like twins, you both wear your one-piece black bathing-suits under your pants; you park and hotfoot it across the sand to the seaweed ridden shore. The waves are tall; they slap against the beach and sound like Alka Seltzer. Marg insists you have to swim since you're here. Marg insists you can't come all this way and not get in any other water other than a sabotaged jacuzzi. So you run in. The water is surprisingly cold, like Canada's. There's an undertow. Seaweed wraps around your neck. You lie back and before a wave capsizes you, Marg snaps your picture. You are wearing thongs and this is mostly what will show up; two sizeable blue floating feet.

Suddenly you scream. Something has brushed against your leg. You spring to your feet. There, undulating in the waves, is an alligator. An anaconda. You scramble to shore. Gradually, the thing washes in. It's a severed tail about five or six feet long. The wound is red, ragged and fresh. The tail tapers off to nothing.

"I think it's a snake," Marg says, captivated.

You look at her. "An anaconda," you say. Once, your brother's girlfriend called your brother's penis the anaconda of love. You told her you weren't interested in knowing.

"Go figure," Marg says, snapping a photo.

Severed, the tail can't do much. It can't do harm. It can't swim. It can't even scare you.

Marg has another idea. She signals and pulls over to the side of the stumpy road and tells you she wants to visit the graveyard. There's a gravestone she wants to show you.

You ought to have guessed this was coming. In all the places you've vacationed in your years together, Marg has wanted to see the graveyards. You think her interest is macabre. You think there is nothing to learn about the Fijian or Mexican population by looking at what kind of

59

graves they make. Marg disagrees. Marg thinks houses of the dead capture the heartbeat of a nation.

"The dead don't have heartbeats," you mutter as she putters onto the thin, asphalt drive snaking through the cemetery. She leaves a sassy plume of blue exhaust behind her. When you pass a high-rise of maybe 40 graves, a condo unit, Marg stops. The graves are indented; they look like cubbyholes for school children. The white stone is blackening with age.

Marg peers at you and says, "You've got me wrong, Joyce."

You are busy trying to knock down the kick stand of your scooter so that you can sidle over to the shade. Your flip flop bends. You bruise your toe and curse. You look up at Marg, who has produced a hanky and is swiping at her high cheekbones, her upper lip, the back of her neck.

"About Emma," she says. "It's not what you think."

You don't know how to respond. You realize that the suspicion of this affair is central to who you've become over the last year.

"She's just a kid I admire."

You know you have to say something. "I love you" is what comes out.

Marg makes a noise in her throat and revs the throttle on her scooter. The bike surges forward; it's an instant more before Marg's torso follows.

It's very hot, very close, and the sun is beating down. The grass here is all scrubby, not really what, in Canada, you'd label grass at all. Of course, Marg and you live in a rainforest, even given the absence of trees. You listen to the surprisingly loud putt-putt of Marg's scooter fade into the distance before you turn the key on your own and try to catch up.

The grave Marg's been trying to show you has this stone: *I Told You I Was Sick*, B. P. Roberts, *May 17, 1929 to June 18, 1979.*

Marg drags you out for a walking tour of Old Key West. There are dozens of houses on the tour but it's too hot to last through all of them. You stand on the sidewalk staring up at assorted homes. While you rub your feet, Marg reads the brochure aloud:

"This is the Richard 'Tuggy' Roberts House," she says. "Two Bahama houses stand side by side. They were originally constructed in the early eighteen-hundreds at Abaco on Green Turtle Cay. In 1846 just after the disastrous hurricane, Joseph Bartlum and Richard Roberts disassembled the buildings and brought sections aboard a sailing vessel to Key West. The scarcity and expense of lumber on this island were key factors for the decision of the master shipbuilders to move the homes."

Marg suggests you stop at Shell World. They have a vast array of conch shells, black coral, shells made into jewellery, salt water taffy and shark jaws. You pick out a conch shell you can hold in your hand; its brown stripes are shiny. You present it to Marg as a token of your trip. All the missing gifts have gone completely out of your head. You can't imagine she would take something you gave her—an emblem of a romantic vacation—and pass it along to a woman with whom, it is clear, she is not having an affair.

It did not occur to you, when you plunked down your money for the sunset cruise, that mostly what you were paying for was the privilege of drinking as much booze as you could pour down your throat. You are a teetotaller and while Marg drinks, she doesn't drink when she's on the water because of vicious seasickness. All the twins, with whom you are in close proximity while the sky dazzles, ignore you steadfastly. The baseball twins are today wearing matched purple tank tops with pink triangles in the spot where, ostensibly, their hearts should be.

"Come on," says Camille, the woman who moved your

luggage from room to room, the one who talked you into this cruise. "Just one drink. It's on me." She orders at the bar then passes each of you an orange concoction that looks nearly dangerous. "Goombay Smashes," she says, "an island tradition."

Obediently, the two of you sip.

You stare at a sign advertising an organization called "reef relief." Accidental boat groundings damage the sensitive reef, it says. "Brown, brown, run aground. Blue, blue, sail on through."

A lone dolphin explodes on the starboard side of the boat, leaping and drawing the boat forward.

You haven't dared to reply to what Marg said in the graveyard. It is too much to hope for, that Marg is faithful, and yet you do hope. At night, in your minute but frozen room, you touch her and tell her you feel like you and she are two halves of the same woman. "Two thirds," you correct.

Marg lifts on her elbow to look at you. She raises her eyebrows. "Goodnight," she says and pushes away your hand.

Before you leave Key West, Marg finds a handmade tile store and talks you into blowing most of your leftover money on two coffee mugs. With the exchange, they cost nearly $100 each. But you think it's a good sign. While they don't exactly match, there are two of them. Two of them. Which must mean that Marg envisions a future for the two of you. You also buy a trivet that depicts a woman and a wolf side by side. You don't say anything out loud, but to yourself you nickname the wolf Emma.

The next afternoon you are off to the alligator farm north of Miami. Your rental car is small, slow, red; in your mind, it flashes your tourist status like a beacon. The Keys are navigable, but once you're north of Key Largo, things are dicier.

You start to notice hurricane damage—palm trees without fronds, mostly. Your mother told you all about Hurricane Andrew, which she watched on CNN, and now you pass what she said along to Marg.

"One woman was in her bedroom with her six-year-old daughter," you say, "and the hurricane swept under the house, pulled up some floorboards and stole the sneaker off the child's foot."

Marg signals a lane change. You want her to say something, but she doesn't.

"A lot of people found out their insurance was no good. The government declared it a disaster area. The hurricane did millions of dollars worth of damage."

Marg adjusts the rear view mirror.

You can't seem to get her attention. You say, "Do you love me?"

She says, "What time does the brochure say this place closes?"

You get lost in Homestead. Homestead is supposed to be one of the most dangerous spots in the Continental US; more people get murdered here than anywhere else. Marg is not impressed with your abilities as a map-reader. You drive up and down country roads that bisect agricultural fields, palm tree nurseries, mostly, but you never find where you're supposed to be going. You say, "Those are Alexandria King Palms they're growing, for your information."

Marg pulls the car over. She reads the map. "This is 192nd Avenue N.W.," she finally says disgustedly. "We're supposed to be looking for S.W. I told you you need reading-glasses."

You say, "Oh. S.W. S.W. Right." You twist the map upside down until S.W. becomes apparent to you.

Marg's patience is being tried. You suggest she let you drive. The only people around are migrant farm workers passing in beat up vehicles. You get behind the wheel where her hands have left wet slicks. She directs you and keeps directing you. Finally, you drive into the slippery edges of sunset.

The Everglades Alligator Farm is the alligator farm closest to the airport, from which, about midnight, you'll leave. It's nearly five. The place closes at six. The dollar-off coupon in your hand is wrinkled and damp, but it still proclaims that you are about to have "A Gatorrific Time!"

"Have you ever been on an airboat?" you ask Marg. Now there are signs that tell you you are getting close: 'Everglades Alligator Farm, 10 miles' and an arrow pointing.

It is very, very rural, but not at all what you imagined the Everglades to look like. You thought of water, swamps, men who wrestled alligators with their bare hands. 'Unspoiled Florida at its Wildest' says the coupon.

You are very tired, very weary, very hot when you pull into the Everglades Alligator Farm driveway. But you're happy to have found it. It's only ten after five, so all the hours of travel, all the stress, has been worth it. On the door to the gift shop is a skeleton with blinking green eyes. Marg puts her face in her hands. You say chirpy things like, "We're here, sweetheart. Come on, my little mung bean. Everything is fine now. You'll see. Let's go have our gatorrific time."

You try to sound upbeat. How did Marg get so far away from you? Because in this Homestead parking-lot, mere feet from thousands of alligators, in a spot not very long ago ravaged by a hurricane more severe than your emotions, you understand that Marg is already gone. She's here, beside you, but she's already gone. If not to Emma, then to whomever her next lover is, to whatever her life holds in store for her future.

Marg looks at you. You try to decipher what's in her eyes. Pity? Her hand reaches for the door. It swings open to blasting heat. You follow her determined walk into the gift shop. Cold air hits you. There are alligator goods arrayed on many glass shelves and for a fleeting second, you're sorry that you spent all your money on art and ceramics. There are alligator stuffed animals and alligator spoons and vinyl alligators that will swing from key chains.

What you'd really like is a picture of someone an alligator chewed up and spit out.

Marg stands in line at the counter. The clerk snaps bubblegum in an otherworldly shade of blue.

"Two," Marg says.

The clerk says, "We're closed." She does something with her register, which is computerized. A register tape begins to jerk out, trailing longer and longer.

Marg says, "You're open till six."

"Sure," says the clerk, "but not for airboat rides. Last airboat ride's at five."

Marg doesn't know what to say. Neither do you. Both of you are imagining this whole insufferable day, the expensive mugs, the hot highways, being frightened and lost in Homestead, driving around aimlessly for hours.

"Come back tomorrow," the clerk tells you. Her eyes slide slowly up and down, up and down, first Marg's body then yours. You'd think she'd never seen lesbians before. The cash register tape winds onto the counter and twists there like something alive, like a snake: an anaconda d'amour.

"We can't," Marg says.

You agree. "We're flying out tonight."

"This is it," Marg says. Marg's haircut is nothing like yours. All those years ago, when you met, it should have been a dead giveaway that the relationship couldn't last.

"She's right," you echo. "This is it."

Karaoke Mon Amour

Mike Barnes

FOREIGN SHAPES

Taiwan is shaped like an egg, an ovary, a tear. Korea is a stubby uncircumcised penis, 1000000 soldiers stationed at its base. Japan is long and gently curving, tapering from a central mass into a chain of ever-smaller islands: it is the seahorse, tail unfurled, floating on ocean currents to the east.

The seahorse (*Hippocampus syngnathidae*) is a marine fish found in shallow tropical or temperate waters. The male develops the eggs and bears the young, incubating them in a brood pouch.

The hippocampus forms a ridge along each lateral ventricle of the brain. It is part of the limbic system, which is involved in the complex physical aspects of behaviour governed by emotion and instinct. The activities governed are those concerned with self-preservation and preservation of the species, the expression of fear, rage and pleasure, and the establishment of memory patterns.

THE TWO SISTERS

English only! was their strict rule at the start, but George soon saw the sense of bending this a little. June, the younger of the two women he tutored on Tuesday, could speak English haltingly—the Taiwanese school system had drilled her mainly in grammar—but her sister, May, could barely speak at all. As they sat around the carved cedar coffee-table, George working with first one sister then the other, it was only natural for June to help out in Mandarin whenever he and May reached an impasse.

The house was May's. Or the first floor was. The basement was rented "to China boy" and the upstairs "to mother, her girl," which partly answered George's puzzlement at how two 30-year-olds with five small children could immigrate and right away purchase a house in North York. Not all of the mystery evaporated. The family business in Taipei seemed modest enough—"we are selling hats," June explained—and May's husband had no regular employment. He practised a martial arts discipline George had never heard of and couldn't pronounce. His trophies stood on the mantel and medals and diplomas hung above them, the only furnishings in the living-room except for the table and the heap of children's toys in a corner. He travelled throughout Asia giving demonstrations. For free? George wondered. He had been gone on one of these junkets since George had met the sisters. Tomorrow he was due back.

"Husband...pick up," May made driving motions in the air.

"I am picking up my husband," George said, writing it at the same time on the paper he would leave behind. "Try."

"Try to say?" May made a comic song of the three words. She said something to June. They both laughed.

"What did she say?" At the question, June blushed and glanced at her sister. May was still laughing, her black eyes glittering.

"He say, your voice sound like music."

George smiled drily, to show he didn't believe that.

67

Some of the paper cranes could sit upright, correctly balanced, but most lay over on one side; some were upside-down. It was as if a strong wind, which neither of them could feel, blew gusts through their apartment. Or perhaps —George had been taken duck hunting as a boy—a flock of the coloured birds had been flying through and had met a hail of gunfire, launched by miniature marksmen hidden among their furnishings.

He showed one to Sonoko, his Friday morning appointment. Shelley made this, he said proudly, bringing out the lime-green crane from a zippered pouch in his briefcase. It was only slightly crushed by his sandwiches.

"Shelley? Ah...your partner." Sonoko spoke with slow precision. She had studied traditional tea ceremony at an institute in Kyoto. Once, when George asked if she would work at that when she returned, her eyes went wide. "I have not served tea for six months." *Out of date?* George thought, before remembering that the whole point of tradition was *never* to go out of date. What did she mean then? That the motions of performing the ceremony were so complex—he imagined slow sequences of turns, clockwise, counter-clockwise, bows, subtle hand gestures—really, he couldn't imagine it. He and Shelley poured water over Lipton.

"This...is...very...lovely," Sonoko said, turning the crane delicately. "Origami. We made in junior school."

"Elementary," George corrected, his armpits flaming for himself as well as Shelley.

KARAOKE

I am in love with someone. He is foreigner. It is impossible to think. I will be insane.

All the way home on the subway, he pressed the pocket

of his shirt, feeling the message on the slip of paper burn against his heart.

But climbing the fire-escape stairs to his apartment, he remembered his friend Howard's words. *These Asian women, they're like western women 40 years ago. Marriage is everything to them. If they don't find a man, they're nothing.* Howard was sexist, reductionist, casually racist; partly for these reasons, George found his company bracing. He pricked balloons. Snug in a regular teaching job, he found George's ESL gigs more amusing than exotic.

Once, in a Forkchops on Bloor, George pressed him to try *kim chi*, the Korean national dish of aggressively spiced cabbage.

Howard, a curry devotee and foreign film fan, was not fazed by the fiery red flecks in vinegar. He chewed a large mouthful judiciously, sweat beading on his forehead.

"They bury it in a pot in the backyard," George told him.

"I believe it," said Howard.

There was a name printed in one very bottom corner of the note, so tiny it looked like a fly's footprints. *Kil Eun-Jee.* He liked the fact that the Koreans seldom picked a western moniker to avoid embarrassing struggles with their names. They let you try. Sometimes, mouthing substitutes like "May" or "June," he felt he was addressing a ghost self, like a hologram, shimmering between himself and the real person.

LOSING BABIES

George reckoned that he and Shelley had lost three children in six months. Shelley felt the same way, though George knew she went too far when she said, as she sometimes did, "It's just like they died." It wasn't *just* like that. As a language teacher he was sensitive to the dangers in the overly literal as well as in the overly metaphorical. Whatever sense he had of a higher power—and it was a very hazy, flickering sense, like early TV—he was sure that it involved at least a fine ear. Talk like that was dangerous. It could get you smacked with some real bad luck.

Not that he and Shelley hadn't had their share. First, they had thought Shelley was pregnant. Finally. Six weeks since her last period, and they had been tossing around names, when her doctor informed her that what she was growing was in fact an ovarian cyst, not a foetus. After her surgery, she was down, lower than even George had ever seen her before. At 39, and with her history of tricky menstruation, her doctor put her chances of another pregnancy at slim. It was George who first contacted the adoption agency. Four years, he was told, if everything went smoothly. Four *years?* He would be 45. Without even mentioning this to Shelley, he made further inquiries and finally found an agency that got—their blunt word—babies from Russia. An agency in Moscow took in homeless babies from all over that vast country, as well as from the former republics, Kazakhstan, Belarus, Georgia. "A clearing house," George thought unwillingly, and saw a van, like an old-style dogcatcher's van, roaming the muddy side streets. "Good health, parents and children," said a crisp young female, who was no less impressive when George met her in person.

Shelley was too depressed still to be very dubious or excited. She acceded.

"Igor? Vasily? Vladimir?" George joked gently, trying to bring her around. He still came home most nights to find her eating nachos in front of Jerry Springer. *Good-Time Grannies: "My Mother Slept With My Son."* She had gained 25 pounds, and was still gaining, even after returning to her part-time hours as a data entry clerk with a survey firm named, unfortunately, Matrix. Their sex life was nil, but had been dwindling for a long time.

"Katerina," she finally said one night with a weak smile. "We can shorten it to Kate."

GOOD FORTUNE

George was disappointed when, after the return of May's husband, May and June cancelled their next two appointments. It was business, partly; they were the last two sessions left in the package of hours they'd bought. But, also, he missed seeing them. He had come to think of the two sisters as an oasis of calm in his week. Peace, and something more. A hint of mystery, and promise of the most relaxing kind, since it need never be fulfilled.

They gave him cups of tea, green or black. Ginger tea once, when he was sick; it was sweet and spicy, the pale root slices floating in the pot, and after each sip it filled the head and chest with a surprising surge of delayed heat. And new food, too: red-bean soup, which he found too sugary. Delicious warm buns filled with green onion or pork bits in a sauce. The house was always silent; strangely silent, for a home to eleven people. But the husband was demonstrating his martial art abroad, the children were at school; even the three tenants had vacated the premises, perhaps in deference to the arrival of "tutor-man," as May sang out when he rang the doorbell. The sense of stolen moments was what made him think of an oasis. The small delight of water and a palm tree, an hour of shade before the march again.

They sat cross-legged around the low, carved coffee table, he on one side, the two sisters on the other. The silence felt to him like another language, a third tongue that murmured between the English and the Mandarin. They laughed a lot. Giggled at mistakes, at deformed vowels and ribald consonants; at bad grammar. Words popped and fizzled and flared like a backyard fireworks display in the air around their heads.

There was an undercurrent. Of course he knew that. It came most forcefully from May, the married one. June was shyer. May would rattle off a string of Mandarin, several sentences worth, which at George's prompting June would translate as, "She feel tired." May, black eyes dancing, looked anything but pooped. He kept asking just to watch June squirm, mumbling the double translation, into a safe lie and then into English.

"Teacher hit," May suggested, holding out her hands when she had failed to do her homework. Her fingers were long and slender, pink from kitchen work, the nails clear and shapely. He felt a buzz of tingling energy in what Howard called "the lowest chakra."

They taught him a Chinese character, which they translated as "Good Fortune." Its difficulty surprised him, 16 strokes in a precise sequence. But then there were quite a few strokes involved in printing "Good Fortune" in English. During lulls in the lesson, he sometimes practised it, May and June laughing delightedly.

Naturally he had fantasies of sleeping with them. Taking the two sisters to bed in the echoing house. Such thoughts never occupied him for long; he enjoyed them in passing. During the first bald patch in their sex life, he and Shelley had visited a therapist, who asked them—five minutes in, which George recognized as a shock tactic—if they "got off on other people." George admitted he did occasionally (often, by that point); and Shelley, tearing up, said she thought she had "once." "Once, schmunz," the therapist, a tough-lover, jeered. He said, "Who cares where you get your appetite, as long as you eat at home." After three sessions they paid their bill and discontinued recovery. They went back to irregular snacking, from their own, or each other's, hands.

The day May's husband returned, there were sounds in the house at last. Deep breathing sounds from the kitchen, like breezes in a poplar grove. George felt nervous. At the end of the session, a squat young man in a burgundy track suit, with a serene boyish face, planted himself in front of him and announced, "I am Dave. I'm happy to meet you." His English was fluent, lightly accented. George wondered why he didn't teach his wife himself. "I would like to speak with you soon."

Soon, George promised.

OUT OF BUSINESS

Often it happened, an almost-expected miracle. "Nature's blessing," the doctor said, then wincing at his own corniness, added that it was probably hormonal. Happy expectation led to the release of endorphins, which stimulated the production of other, ah.... George heard confusion and perhaps ignorance in the too-rapid delivery. But it didn't matter. Shelley was smiling. Suddenly, two babies were on the way. Vladimir-Katerina would be joined by Michael-Rebecca.

They would love them equally.

But, actually, both babies took a detour and wound up somewhere else. The Russian baby agency, or Canada's branch of it, went out of business. *This number is no longer in service,* said a sexy female voice each time George called. Then they received a registered letter from a lawyer's office saying that their deposit had been seized as evidence pertaining to a police investigation and would be returned when, and if, etc. Vladimir-Katerina was stuck in Vitebsk or Kustanaj or Batumi. George didn't know why, but it made him feel better to find these names in the atlas, give him/her a dot in the countryside at least. Michael-Rebecca went down the toilet, a spontaneous first trimester abortion. "Go down the toilet" was one of the idioms he taught his students for a project failing; "go down the tubes" was another. It was the horrible accidental exactness of language, no less than our fumbling attempts to control it, that oppressed him often.

Shelley didn't cry, not once that he saw. Her gently sorrowing face frightened him more than a Hallowe'en mask. She watched Seinfeld, Springer and Sally with unwavering attention, but was hazy on details when he asked her the retention-testing questions he had developed in his work.

EAT SNOW

When he asked his students what they had done on the weekend, the answer, if not "study English," was usually "karaoke." George had once joined a group that bellowed "Proud Mary" at a smear of cheering faces in a northern roadhouse serving half-price draft and chicken wings. That was fifteen years ago. Shelley had been one of the other drunken singers, swaying in a line with arms linked about each other's waists. He hadn't known her name yet. Six months later, they were living together.

But the Asian karaoke experience was, he gathered, different. "You must join us on a weekend, I insist," said Dae-Jung, a stylish architect from Seoul whom he met for "grammar refinement."

George was drunk by midnight when they reached the bar. Pitchers of draft were sloshing on top of a slithery supper of noodles topped with, first, a fried egg, then a glutinous black bean sauce. Tasty enough, though a bit much for his chopstick technique. The six Koreans, three of them clients, laughed good-naturedly. Shelley had begged off. Outside Christie station, George saw signs in Korean, the oblongs and circles less angular than Chinese characters. "Korean town," said the slight girl with the sombre, almost grieving expression who had been sitting next to him at dinner. He had forgotten her name, but at the hint of irony in her voice, he smiled.

74

Concrete stairs led down into the karaoke bar. Opium dens, George thought. It was not officially licensed, but at a word from Dae-Jung, the manager dipped below the counter and came up with a twelve-pack of Coors. An assistant showed then to one of the rooms. It was small, with clean white walls; an L-shaped black mock-leather couch faced the electronics stand in the corner; between them, a coffee-table with the songbooks, a remote and two microphones. Faint thumps and laughter could be heard through the walls. Sex hotel, thought George, renting rooms by the hour.

The three girls were giggling as they flipped through the Korean and Chinese songbooks. He opened the English one. "Moon River," "What's New Pussycat?" and "Do Ya' Think I'm Sexy?" Obviously selection was going to be a problem. "I insist you choose," pressed Dae-Jung, standing with mike in hand. He hit the dimmer switch and a small mirror ball in the corner began spinning, spraying dots of primary colours through the dusk. The lights spattered over and around the stand with its winking numbers, not quite reaching to where they sat. Electronics are the star, George thought; we have to emulate them.

Dae-Jung punched in the numbers of a Korean song. He blended seamlessly into the mix. So did the next two singers, each of them delivering a song without a glitch. That spooked George; he had been expecting a sing-along, but this was more like lip-syncing. Another problem was the accompaniment, not the original tracks minus the vocals, as long ago in the roadhouse, but a peppy Muzak, heavy on synth and programmed rhythm tracks. The videos featured beautiful Asian women in filmy clothes, striking poses in front of a backdrop of stone columns, ocean sunset or floral wallpaper.

Dae-Jung was pointing with the mike. George scanned the titles hopelessly. That was when he spied "Come Together" and remembered its tonic weirdness.

In the far corner of the black couch, the thin sad girl was

staring at him. Grief and longing sloshed behind the mini-portholes of her glasses. No-one sat very close to her. She had not sung, would not now.

With a sigh amplified into Apple wind, he began:

Here come ol' flat-top
he come groovin' up slowly
he got Joo Joo eyeball
he one holy roller
He got hair down to his knee
got to be a joker, he just do what he please

For once, the group didn't laugh or clap loudly. After he finished rasping, a smattering of polite applause dispelled the silence. Dae-Jung clapped him on the back and launched into "Don't Be Cruel." He had a nice, light tenor.

Sometime toward the end of the evening, George had sung a few songs and drunk a few more beers, he was getting into it, not caring any more, when he heard a voice in his ear, at first he thought it came from inside his head, a woman's voice murmuring, "I like your deep voice. I wanna'—" Was he hallucinating? Around the urgent whisper, he heard a thin male voice, climbing an alien melody over a pounding beat.

He looked to his left and saw the grieving girl staring at her hands folded in her lap. He thought he saw her lips move—a silent prayer? She got up suddenly and left the room.

A short time later, he found himself on the street. New snow had fallen. The other faces looked as dizzy, as reeling under the streetlights, as he felt himself. The thin girl was looking away; she seemed impatient now, like someone waiting for a ride that is late. In the shuffle of going she had slipped a note into his pocket that he could feel with his fingers. A girl was scooping up snow and pushing it at her boyfriend's face. "Here, eat snow!"

Shelley had learned to make the origami cranes from a home decorating show on the Life Network. The show's host was a sort of Canadian Martha Stewart, less finicky and less impressive; often her instructions trailed off in a hazy "...or whatever." After she taught the viewers how to fold them, she showed the finished cranes to her gardening specialist, who happened to be Japanese.

"Ah...lovely," he said, as Sonoko had told George. He went on to relate the Japanese custom of making 1000 of the cranes as a form of prayer, for someone who was sick, for instance. He didn't mention that the technique was learned in elementary school.

"Wow! Well, if you're not up to 1000, you can always enclose one in a Get Well card, since they flatten right out, or on a gift, or whatever," bubbled the host.

Shelley bought sheets of coloured paper which she cut into two-inch squares. She had sheets of many colours: grass green, cedar green, ruby red, sky blue, cobalt blue, cotton candy pink, butter yellow, tangerine, burgundy. Deep, rich colours. She made a special expedition to the Japanese Paper Store to get sheets of gold and silver. These were George's favourites; they glittered like a king's ransom.

When folding the cranes, Shelley worked her way through all of the colours before returning to the first one. It was her own superstition. She did not use white or, of course, black.

At first, George knew, she was folding the cranes as a prayer for a healthy baby. She had seen the decorating show when her period was four weeks overdue. When that baby turned out to be a fibrous growth, he thought she must be folding the cranes for herself, substituting her name for the baby's in her prayer. He reminded her of the doctor's lack of concern, which they should interpret as reassurance. Finally he got up nerve to ask her.

"No," she said, folding deftly by now. "I want a baby."

All through the successive fiascos that followed, the loss of two more babies, each loss more actual, and thus more painful, than the one before, Shelley kept folding the cranes. By now George was confused about the reason, and to pray without purpose made him vaguely uneasy. Coloured cranes perched on the bookcase, the table, the fridge. They filled glass jars and bowls. Inevitably, with the wind of someone passing, they littered the floor, snagged in dust balls. George began to worry that they were unlucky.

"You didn't actually 'lose' the babies," said Howard over lunch one day. Then, remembering, he added, "Except for the miscarriage, of course." He didn't blush at his gaffe, though George winced inwardly; in his private sociology he had noticed that film buffs were not as easily embarrassed as most people.

"We didn't win," he said, demoting his feeling to irony. He thought that he had gone further than Howard in plumbing the meaning of loss. Loss was any missed chance or opportunity. It was the perception of absence, specific or generalized. It carried with it feelings, not only of sadness and anger, but also guilt and confusion, blurred identity. Sometimes he felt he must have misplaced the babies; they would turn up if he only looked hard enough. Other times he felt that the babies were right where they belonged, and he was the one who had got turned around. He was a wanderer in a vast labyrinthine city, and he couldn't find a map or properly ask for directions. He couldn't even remember where he was staying, or who he was supposed to meet. Had the babies sensed that in advance and avoided such a befuddled dad?

"You don't have to see it all the way through," he said to Shelley one night. He had decided she was in superstitious thrall to a number, 1000, and maybe he could help her free herself.

"No!" Her face filled with a foreboding he had never seen

in it before. "I don't want us to lose any more."

So she did have a prayer. Not for gain, but against loss. Any, all, loss? And when she finally gave up folding, was that, he wondered, final resignation? He preferred to think it was boredom. Boredom was the commonest kind of bad faith.

But he wished she had given up earlier, or else finished the job. 737 miniature coloured cranes, constituting just over two-thirds of a prayer: that seemed like a definition of bad luck.

WHAT HAPPENED AT THAT THEATRE?

Some events are stubbornly surreal. It is as if they exist in an alternate universe and resist all our efforts to drag them into this one. All we glimpse here is odd, off-kilter limbs, sudden gasps, bits of a reality that somewhere else, perhaps, is correctly proportioned and breathing comfortably. It was like that the time George took Sonoko to the movies.

It began the night before, when he phoned to ask her. "Hel-lo...hel-lo?" she kept saying, as if they had a bad connection. Then, dubiously, "George?" They had been meeting once a week for three months, but this was the first time he had phoned her. Occasionally she called him, to cancel or reschedule.

After a pause, Sonoko said, "It would be...Dutch treat?" "Good," George said, "yes."

They met outside the Cumberland theatre. Sonoko's normally pale face was chalk white, her black hair pinned back severely. She wore a long, black wrinkled raincoat. He thought of Pound's lines: "The apparition of these faces in the crowd/Petals on a wet, black bough." She had also studied kabuki theatre; not performing it, of course, only men did that. But as they paid for the tickets, he looked closely at her face, believing he saw a layer of fine white

79

powder blend with warmer tones at her neckline. A sweet-ish smell rose from around her.

The ticket-seller and his companion—the manager?—were middle-aged men who George assumed were gay. They were well-groomed and they spoke in quiet voices, their heads close together. It made the bare lobby strangely cozy, so unlike the brisk hetero exchange—a boy or girl barking "Next"—at most box offices. The ticket-taker also seemed homosexual, perhaps just by association, but his personality was rougher, less composed. A high school dropout beside university graduates, thought George, con-figuring things. He was also a bit younger.

"Ah, you're going for the real stuff."

The ticket-taker spoke so quickly that Sonoko frowned in puzzlement. Even George barely understood the blur of syllables.

"If it weren't for live flesh none of us would be here."

The comments seemed torn out of context, and George was sitting down before they made any sense. The movie they were seeing was "Live Flesh," directed by Pedro Almodovar from a novel by Ruth Rendell. Waiting in the dusk, he smelled Sonoko's perfume, stronger at close quarters, a cloying scent with something faintly metallic, a faint iron smell, underneath. Sonoko was too fastidious ever to permit body odour. George thought idly of sleeping with her, her strong legs—she rock-climbed as fiercely as she memorized verbs—cinched around his back. Partly this was automatic, having sexy thoughts before movies. It was the dark, the screen about to come alive, the nearby strangers.

A woman's scream began the movie. Briskly an older woman bundled her into an off-duty bus where she gave birth to a baby boy.

Sonoko leaned close to whisper something.

"Erotic?" he guessed.

"No!" Fiercely. "I know 'erotic.' Exotic."

The helpful woman used the driver's shoelaces to tie off

the umbilical cord, and then, having nothing else sharp, she bit through it with her teeth. She sat in the seat behind the mother, her mouth red-smeared, like her hands and the baby she cradled. Tennyson's red-toothed, red-clawed nature. That was unusual in movies; usually newborns were shown born pink and glowing, as if bathed and talcumed prior to entry. The mother groaned deeply. "Keep pushing, it's the placenta," the impromptu midwife advised. George heard another soft gasp.

It was Sonoko. He turned to see her face floating ghost-like, drained and stricken. At once he understood her perfume with its ferrous undertone and the enhanced pallor of her face. It would be like Sonoko, with her blended masochism, to cover the evidence of her period with minis-trations that actually drew attention to it. Mishima, he recalled, was her beloved author.

"Excuse me," Sonoko squeezed past without touching him. She never returned.

Afterwards he felt disjointed but refreshed, which from what Howard had told him was standard for an Almodovar movie. Shelley was in bed sleeping when he got home. He climbed in beside her and began stroking the small of her back. She responded slowly, with sleepy moans. Guilty but horny, he persisted. He came to a vision of Sonoko wearing a strap-on, fucking the sad Korean girl in the ass.

Who cares where you get your appetite.

"What happened at that theatre?" Shelley murmured before returning to sleep. He had told her that much.

ASSHOLE

Dave was doing his breathing exercises in the kitchen next to the living-room. George could hear him as he finished with the two sisters. He sounded like a soft engine starting up. Husbands, George thought, and wondered who would

81

be more hopeless: a TSN addict who spent his days on the couch, or a martial arts expert who stood in rooms flexing and breathing. June poured more tea.

"My country is beautiful, yes," Dave was saying. George had asked about his trip. "It is my country. But it is crowded. Con...compressed? No. Congested?" George nodded. "Europeans called it Formosa."

Dave smiled as he spoke, a winning, boyish smile that lit up his handsome face. But George knew that he put too much stock in smiles. He always had; it was a weakness. He couldn't recognize aggression easily unless it came accompanied by scowls and grimaces and glares. But usually it didn't.

"I always called it Taiwan," George said.

May and June had moved back discreetly from the table. They were standing a few feet away, their faces meek and expectant.

"You are a great language teacher." George grinned at the exaggeration. "I am also a teacher. I could show you something."

Which is how George found himself standing rock-still in the centre of the living-room for several long minutes, trying to relax and "go heavy" as instructed, feeling stiffness and soreness and restless energy migrate around his body. Feeling aches and pains. Feeling idiotic as he stared straight ahead out the window at the street, catching blurs of May and June and Dave moving around him, observing him as one would a museum exhibit. *Toronto man, 1998.*

Dave had shown him the place on the balls of his feet where the weight was supposed to concentrate. He told him the name, which George pronounced and forgot. By now he had great difficulty learning anything he knew he would never use. Dave's instructions were to "relax...go heavy," let all his weight flow down through the balls of his feet. Back into the earth. George tried. Then—having read some Zen in his time—he tried not to try. Dave moved around him like a tailor, prodding him in the shoulder and stomach and thigh and buttocks. George was shamed by the mushiness of his muscles, but Dave muttered "Not tight …let go." Finally, George succeeded in the sense that his various aches and pains merged into a general discomfort, and the energy of his body was concentrated mostly in his brain. He wondered if the froth of pink in the yard was a cherry tree. That would be almost as good as a lotus blossom. He also wondered what the best word would be for the way he felt, standing still in a living-room among moving, watching people, his mouth falling open whenever he forgot about it.

He decided the best word would be asshole.

Finally it was over. Dave looked at his watch. "Five minutes. Okay. Do it every day until you can do fifteen minutes. Very relaxed. If you feel pain, sudden pains, stop immediately."

"I will," George promised.

May and June were watching him seriously. It was a pleasure to be able to move his head again—that relaxed him. Soon he would leave and that made him feel warmly about May and June, the times they'd had together. He looked back at Dave and almost gasped. Dave's mouth was open, his eyes glazed; his arms hung limply at his sides and he leaned forward at a dangerous angle. He looked like a corpse tied to a stake. After a moment, George realized that he was being shown the correct procedure. He felt his own posture sag at the thought that the demonstration was not over.

"Feel my chest," the corpse murmured.

George put his hand on Dave's chest. It felt plump and still. "Through your stomach?" he guessed.

"Feel my stomach."

More plump stillness. Despite himself, George was curious.

"I'm breathing through my——." The word for the balls of his feet. George nodded, as he did when a street person told him he could fly.

After watching for another minute or so—seeing nothing more—George said that he had to go. He bent to get his briefcase. "Let me show you something," he heard as fingers gripped his upper arm. Anger spread like a rash over his skin. Now he was being detained.

"Stand there," Dave said. He turned George's shoulders and positioned his feet so that George was advancing on him partly in profile, like a boxer. Standing very close, an inch away, he snuggled up with his head on George's breastbone. He adopted his limp posture, breathing through—, his hands falling like soft plumb weights against George's forward thigh.

"Now push me," he mumbled.

George knew what was coming. Any man would. But he pushed anyway.

The result was still amazing. It was like pushing a rag doll weighing 300 pounds. Dave felt soft and slippery, George could barely get a grip on his shoulders, as if he had been rolled in butter and then bolted to the floor. Despite himself, he pushed harder, straining. The head lolled against his chest, the small massive body rotated barely. The two sisters snickered. George felt duly humiliated and also, strangely, that this was deserved. "Push harder," said the other man. George stopped pushing.

SLUGFEST

"What kind of a name is Kill?"

"Just one 'l'." George usually did the laundry, but Shelley had been emptying his shirt pockets—why? he wondered—and had found the note Kil Eun-Jee had passed him at the karaoke bar.

"Whatever."

"It's just a name. Like Smith."

84

"Smith is like Kill?" They were looking at two different names in their heads, and he couldn't change her spelling. She had her hands on her hips.

"It is if you don't know the words."

A simmering silence followed. They retreated to opposite corners of the small apartment. Like most long-time couples, they argued with the practiced rhythms of boxers, in rounds with inviolable rest periods in between. The combat itself took many forms: dancing, feinting, jabbing, slugging, hugging and resting. Or someone could drop his or her gloves suddenly, inexplicably, inviting the knockout punch.

"What do you think of me?" She was standing in the doorway. Why did she have to be in a doorway? he thought, with a sudden opaque fear. He put down what he had been doing, writing cheques to various creditors, while she repeated her naked question.

What right did he have to speak the truth? Lying seemed more defensible at the moment. But he began anyway. "You've let yourself go." An emptiness, a soft vacancy, came into her face. "At times you seem to have given up already. At 39." He could feel himself using these complaints as ladder rungs to climb toward an impossible statement. Finally he reached it. "I don't love you anymore." It had to be the truth.

She went to her sister's in Brampton. At least it was closer to where she worked. Her new smile was soaked in irony. There had been no more scenes after the last one.

WORD-OF-MOUTH

Dave was smiling broadly. "Each of us is a master of his own—" He sought for a word and then gestured at June. She knew it. "Discipline," Dave repeated.

They were standing by the front door. George had his coat on.

"You can learn any language," Dave declared, with how much intentional absurdity George could only guess.

He groped behind himself for the doorknob. Then, on impulse, he opened his briefcase and retrieved a piece of paper and a pen. Quickly and accurately, he made the series of strokes May and June had taught him. "Good fortune," he said, handing it to Dave.

Dave was a controlled man. His only reaction was the abrupt extinction of his smile, as if a candle had been blown out. It came back, but flickeringly, beset by an inner breeze. He turned and went down the hall.

George felt the brass of the doorknob, a cold globe; he just had to turn it. May and June were whispering, darting hurt glances up at him. Well, he had betrayed them. He knew, in a general way, what the character must mean, even if he couldn't translate it exactly. *Fuck? Fuck me?* Probably it was less aggressive, almost innocent. *Sex. Make baby.*

Then Dave was coming back, his face dense as a stormcloud. He advanced swiftly upon them. George assumed he was about to be given the complete demo.

What Dave did, in fact, was hand him his business card. Characters and numbers on a cardboard rectangle. *Fax* and a number added in pen. George inclined his head, but had nothing to give in return. He had no card. His business was strictly word-of-mouth.

With a groan of relief, he sealed himself in his car and switched on the ignition, windshield wipers and Mix 99 (Oldies and The New). The eastern peace. He had to admit he didn't understand it. The comfortably slumped body, the calm eyes, took on another aspect as he watched them in memory. What he was seeing looked very much like what he would call stubbornness. Could it be a basic difference between east and west? He considered the possibility cautiously. Prejudice and stereotypes lay that way, but perhaps some truth as well. He was a western man, desperate to fly by any means, guile definitely not excluded, and as he drove down the drizzling road he puzzled over why anyone would deliberately court the forces pulling him back to earth.

FRIENDS

Howard had been a lot of things. Had started being a lot of things anyway. A film studies major. A law student. He was one of those who become a teacher in order to have a steady platform from which to make leaps into the unknown, certain he will land somewhere safe again. Grey-haired now, he was thinking of applying for medical school. "Before the door closes." These days, there were some Doc U's that counted life experience almost as much as marks.

One day in May, George met him for coffee at the Manu-Life Centre. They sat at a wobbly little table with their cappuccinos. "Okay, so play doctor," George said.

"What do you mean?"

"C'mon, I know you. What've you been reading?" George did know Howard. "Reading up," in its preliminary phase of dreaming and loose associations, was what he did best, what he started things for.

Howard looked sheepish. "Geez." Then, with a frown of retrieval, he was off. "Well, I've been doing some reading on neurology. Brain anatomy and function. There's this little gizmo called the 'hippocampus' which is sort of a mystery. I mean, it's involved in higher and lower functions in ways nobody understands exactly. The name comes from the Latin for seahorse. Actually, the Greek: 'hippos,' horse, and 'kampos,' monster. Some of those early anatomists must have been pretty wired to see a seahorse in a little bulge of grey matter."

Howard paused, and took a long sip of warm coffee.

87

"You sound like a doctor," George said, untruthfully. A doctor would have bypassed the whimsical etymology and the wired anatomists for the serious memory work. Howard relaxed visibly. His shoulders sagged with a naturalness that would have pleased Dave.

"How's Shelley doing?" he asked.

George hesitated, then confided in the pseudo-doctor.

"I feel guilty, somehow."

"In what sense?"

"In the sense—" What was the sense? "In the sense of collaborating with the forces bringing her down."

"That sounds pretty abstract."

"It isn't. Not at all."

They left soon after that. Howard had himself on a schedule and had to get back to studying. George walked along Bloor Street; paper litter was eddying in semi-tropical funnels of air. Leaving friends, he often felt vaguely depressed. He made friends quickly, had found them wherever he lived; but, after seeing them, his dominant impression was of not knowing, or being known by, them. At times this could feel invigorating. It was like the bitter freedom he had sniffed reading Camus for the first time. But that was twenty years ago, and nowadays the scent was more elusive, its hints more apt to frighten than inspire.

HOMELAND

The coloured cranes, which he moved to safe places but did not discard, were like confetti thrown at the marriage of need and speed. He thought of the jets whizzing overhead, full of tourists, businessmen, students, the intercontinental flux. Seekers in their early twenties who thought nothing of stopping in Toronto *on their way* to Europe. The planet was small, but wind-swept.

He took out his date book. The last page was graffitied

with phone numbers. He looked at them, not sure which was the one he needed. The numerals swam, changed places. Finally he tried one:

Hello. I have returned to my homeland. If you want to talk to me you can reach me there. I hope you will contact me.

The hiss of tape unspooling after this was not a mistake. George realized this as he listened to it. The moving silence was full of whispers, of ghost voices, a conversational wind, decipherable if one had the key. Patience was the key, as was desire. Something else? No-one had forgotten anything.

The Sky-Coloured Boat

François Bonneville

At the rim of a park of a half-dozen tired mobile homes, Turner Linka smoked a roll-me-own. He beheld the creek before him that only this April had surged with violence from the Rockies. Brown water had hardly kept to past seasons' winding gouges. In a confused garter snake of a pattern. Eastern Colorado. So damn flat, Turner mused, how's water to figure out what's down?

Instead of living in Greeley with most of the other grad students, Turner had preferred dome-skied solitude if he so chose, along with something he romantically termed "real life." The commute had grown tedious soon enough, but he did find a poker game he liked with cowfolks hereabouts, plus you couldn't beat just sitting and smoking and pencilling sketch after sketch of plants.

It was June now. No classes for the summer. The creek no longer flowed but shone glazed at its bed. "In a couple of weeks," a poker player had told him, "all you'll get out of there is more dust to the wind." But for now.... Brilliant in the sun.... Turner strolled into the creekbed, skirted a puddle and came to rest his wrists on low-bent knees. He'd have to squint to see anything. He chucked his cigarette and pulled forward the frayed straw brim of his hat.

The creekbed soon revealed itself not smooth but as cracked porcelain, each dark facet lighter and upturned at the edges. Turner broke out his lens, and now the mudcakes loomed lush with blue-green algae, mosses, germinating seeds of desert daisies.... He carefully penknifed one of the cakes loose. A small, shiny blue-and-red wasp escaped. A beetle chose not to budge. Turner carried the cake toward the bank and his trailer where he'd view it through a microscope and identify some mosses. He was 26, blond, hooknosed and gangle-limbed. He'd have Asian eyes if they weren't so grey. One last look down the mud-gully of the creek, a slow, pungent draught into his nostrils, and for no reason he could figure, he sensed a tug at his groin muscles.

Turner had cheered to his new home all spring. The rent was cheap, and he loved compact utility. He loved pretending he dwelled in a train. With plywood he'd fashioned a deep horseshoe of table reaching three walls of the master room at the rear. One castered swivel-chair, and he could flit from drawing pad to computer keys to boxes of twigs he'd sampled. Opposite bud scale scars.... Alternating ones.... Bix Biederbecke on the CD player.... These days, though, the trailer was plain too hot, and evenings offered later and later reprieve until more than one morning he woke up (alone as usual these days), unblanketed, naked and spreadeagled, yet all sweaty still. He gave up locking the place and left all doors and windows broad.

After dinner one Tuesday he was smoking instead of doing dishes, rolling a cold can of beer across his forehead when a large, laden pickup drew into the drive next door. That trailer, white with vestiges of peach and aqua trim, had sagged vacant for months, and now it echoed peeps and gutturals and hardly-hears as a family spilled into it. The pickup looked recent under its dirt. Minnesota plates. Deep cab with back seat. Packed high and unwieldy, its load of household goods was covered by a blue, wooden boat upside down and roped every which way to rear bumper and brackets at the sides.

"There goes the solitude," Turner laughed to himself,

though not without some bitterness at exactly that. Here six months and already claiming earshot privileges. Stop somewhere long enough and tradition makes it yours. When card players had referred to him, "Hey, new guy, your deal," or "What's with the new guy, huh? Never heard of seven-stud bandito?" he'd argued the reverse:

"Excuse me, but I'm not exactly the youngest one here. The time a body's been alive is not that big a deal, I'll admit—but it's a lot less tenuous a marker of one self than a spot where you might try your luck on a rolling, drifting planet."

The card table had gone quiet after that one.

Next door the family unloaded suitcases, boxes, an ironing-board, a weed whacker.... Turner popped the beer can open and took a swig. Oh well.... No longer the new guy around here, that part of things had its appeal.

Plus it wasn't long before the new new guy, likely husband of one and father of two, nicely demonstrated how to cob a trailer cool. Every day in his clean, pressed shirt, the man would turn on the sprinkler he'd centred on his roof, and as steam rose from the sheet metal, Turner could just imagine home-heat drawing up with it. He'd have to copy that. Acknowledgment first. Stepping out of his van one time, he chinned toward the sprinkler and said "Great idea" to the man, though all he got back was an abstracted "What? Oh. That...."

The kids wouldn't engage in a chat with Turner either. They had the same face as the mother, oblong, eyes wide apart, the face somehow never in profile but full front like an old Slavic icon. Full front but looking elsewhere. The teenaged boy power-chorded an electric guitar, astride its amp in the yard. The girl, five or maybe eight (Turner couldn't figure little kids' ages), posed doll after doll on the wooden steps to the kitchen door. Black, ghoulish chested T-shirt for the boy. Wide pink-and-white stripes atop a fuchsia skirt by the stairs. Lacy white ankle socks. The father might exit their kitchen, nearly trip on the dolls, stop, breathe a while and sidestep them. He mowed the yard once with a bright Craftsman machine. A slit of a lawn. Ten swaths, maybe. A week later he removed the weight-bricks and plastic from the mower, but the lawn hadn't grown but browned somewhat already, a neon pink bicycle here, the amplifier, a croquet set, a green-and-yellow rake, fluffy baseball and bat, the sky-coloured boat leaned over the trailer hitch, its snub nose up to a window-screen.... The man yanked at the starter rope. Weakly so. The mower didn't churn first try, and he covered it again. Instead he rerouted the hose and soaked his boat.

Every evening he hosed his boat. He'd depart early in the mornings and return mid-afternoon. His wife might fill the cab with laundry and drive to the coin-op then. You seldom saw the two of them talk.

The poker game moved to Turner's trailer for a while.

"When's your own sprinkler rig going up?" a stubble-faced player wondered. "Promises, promises...."

"Hurry up and lose so I can afford it," Turner told him.

Turner's older brother Chris landed a rented, single-engined Cessna 172, high-winged with struts, in the local strip of oiled dirt. He lived with their mother in Boulder where he retailed restaurant equipment, comfortable enough to take off now and then and fish Wyoming, Montana, the wily trout. Chris offered everyone a share of batter-fried fish and joined the poker game. Even in tartan shirt and jeans he looked like he was wearing a suit. The locals kept comparing Turner to him and poking fun.

"...How come you got all the good looks, Chris?"

"...Too bad being gainfully employed doesn't run in the family, don't you think?"

Turner didn't say much for a while. He didn't notify his brother how sometimes you could see his cards mirrored in those aviator shades.

"Funky digs you've got here," Chris scanned and said. "Ronica like it?"

"That's over," Turner tersely answered him.

"Oh, yeah? She still calls Mom...."

"Who's Ronica?" the stubble-faced player asked.

"Two bits is the bet," a retired gunsmith said.

The stubble-faced player winked. "Ronica, huh? Guess now we won't have to wonder."

Chris looked out the window and wanted to know what earthly good a rowboat could accomplish where there wasn't a river or pond for a hundred miles.

The table chuckled.

The neighbour hosed his boat.

"Two bits is the bet," the gunsmith repeated.

Chris allowed how with a putt-putt motor the boat might be fun. "Closer to where I live, maybe."

The gunsmith tapped his fingers. "That's two bits to stay in," he insisted, and everyone folded.

"You got any *real* music?" a ranch hand asked Turner who sighed back, "Nope. Nothing dripping with sadness and regret, I'm afraid."

The players had heard the story before about that student in Turner's biology lab, but they liked it and watched for Chris' reaction.

It seemed that sometime in January, Turner was familiarizing his freshmen with the basics of the microscope. Each was to run a toothpick across the inner cheek to dislodge some squamous epithelia cells, deposit them onto a slide and observe them. One girl raised her hand. Neither she nor her partner could figure out what these things wriggling in the liquid might be. Turner had a look. He told the girl not to worry about it; the class wouldn't be covering those for a while. He removed the slide and issued her partner a new one to try out, then once the lab was over, he gathered some fellow assistants to check out the still-live sperm.

"No!" blurted Chris.

"That's a definite yes."

"No way."

"Oh, it's so, all right," the stubble-faced player offered.

And the ranch hand: "You don't just make shit like that up."

"Well, you don't know my brother."

The table looked to Turner.

His eyes tilted down-angled, a gracious threat of hurt.

"My friends," he shrugged, "this kind of imagination, I don't have."

"Whatever you say."

Turner lobbed in his ante.

"There's no accounting for blood, is there?"

"Cards, gentlemen?" Chris shuffled the deck and dealt.

Earlier and earlier in the afternoons, the driveway gravel next door crackled under the big pickup's tires. One time the man stumbled sidling out of his cab, then from inside the trailer argument sounds rose. It was the most Turner had heard of the woman's voice to try and make out her words.

"Enough," she said. "Enough. Enough. Enough."

The boy shuffled outside. He sat on a stair and hugged his guitar. The man drove off again and didn't moisten his boat that evening.

Next noon it was the boy who turned on the roof sprinkler.

Three days running the boat leaned unwatered under the sun. Then the following morning Turner perceived past the rim of his Las Vegas coffee mug, through the dust of his slatted window and into the still, dry air, that something wasn't the same.

No truck. No sounds. No people. The peach-and-aqua trailer door hung open.

Turner rolled a cigarette, refilled his coffee and stepped

outside.

The amplifier and bicycle were gone, and so were the dolls, the mower and the croquet set, but the weed whacker stuck out from under the trailer still, the fuzzy bat remained (no ball), the hose, the wooden boat.... From the doorway Turner made out a Yahtzee box inside, the ironing-board, clothes, waxed paper plates on the linoleum. Ash fell from his cigarette into his mug. He flung the coffee to the grass.

After breakfast he had a hard time focusing on plant life. He couldn't read beyond any given paragraph. If he put the book down, he'd find himself dwelling on Ronica. How she didn't abide his cigarettes. How the notion of having children with him took hold of her until she just wasn't a pleasure anymore. Nor was sex with her after a while because he couldn't put it past the urgency of her to up and skip her pills. What did he know? She was pretty and alluring and kind to old folks and all. Maybe she wouldn't. But he'd heard tell of subterfuge like that, and the way Ronica's eyes focused not on his but into the air between them sometimes, only one side of her mouth in smile and the rest of her imperative, unfathomably inside herself, he'd had to admit she scared him.

He ended up playing a computer game of Desperate Goths until eleven or so when he sharpened his penknife, opened and closed his fridge more than once, sat at the toilet, then loped next door, disconnected the hose and sprinkler and parked them under his trailer. He took the weed whacker too, he didn't know what for. Inside the place he filled a box with two red-and-gold ashtrays, a stapler that could probably be fixed, an unopened can of Diet Coke, a shower curtain for drop-cloth use and some cotton shirts for rags. The paper plates would hold samples nicely.

Momentum might've had him take the boat too, but he slowed himself. He ran a hand down the flat bottom of it, its frayed strip of keel, then he pulled its nose from the trailer screen and lowered it to the gravel. A made-in-a-home-workshop craft. Not sky-coloured on the inside but navy blue. Ten feet long, he figured. What might've been one more foot to bring its bow to a point had been squared off instead. A middle seat with oar locks in the gunwales. (No oars nearby that he'd noticed.) A wraparound bench aft. A reinforced stern to hold a motor's clamps. It had no smell. Even close up when Turner squatted to it.

No more use to me than to that guy, he decided. Still, he'd phone and ask Chris if maybe he wanted it.

"What, the putt-putt thing?" wondered Chris.

"Everybody took off."

"Jesus, huh? Hey, Turn, you don't shower for a couple of months, you know, you won't ever keep a neighbour."

"You want the boat?"

"Yeah. Sure. Drive it down sometime."

"No, come get it," Turner told him. "I'm busy these days."

"I'm sure you are. Still ogling that squiggling sperm?"

"That'd be dried and very dead by now."

"Your own, then?"

"You want the boat or not?"

"Yeah, yeah.... Water it till I show, all right?"

"When?"

"The weekend.... Saturday...." Chris promised. "By the way, you gonna call Mom sometime?"

"If she ever figures out I'm not twelve years old."

"Maybe you are," Chris told him.

The neighbour's door stayed open until regular dusk-hour rains from the Rockies' foothills made it this far east one time. Turner went out and latched it then. His brother didn't show that weekend, and Turner ended up driving halfway to Boulder. In a diner parking-lot, they slid the boat into Chris's *Colorado Restaurant Supply* cab-over truck.

Turner minded the new scratches on his van, which already bore its share.

"Who's the friggin twelve-year-old," he muttered.

Summertime waxed.

The sprinkler-on-the-roof method ended up working well enough. It rendered tolerable the heat, though July still dried a slice of bread left two minutes out of the bag.

In the creekbed, algae had turned amber, crusted opalescent, then yielded to the wind. The mudcakes were powder now too. A scorpion under a rock kept Turner and his camera busy one afternoon until, straw hat between him and the sun or not, he sensed nascent warblings of a fever. He'd kept a few mudcakes moist in the fridge, and at the microscope, he wasn't 100% sure, but he might just have discovered an unclassified moss. If so, he'd get to name it. The poker players might get a yuck if he asked them for suggestions. Or else he wouldn't. How might one latinize Bix Biederbecke?

Someone apprised the owner of the park that that family had up and left. The landlady's name was Dixie. Dixie Schneider. Her hair's stiff flip made her look as if she'd ribboned half a violin to her head.

"Mister Linka," Dixie wanted to know. "You fixing to grow your own lawn up there?"

No matter how Turner whined about how the neighbour had been sprinkling his roof the same way for weeks, there was no dissuading her that water in these parts couldn't be frittered away like that.

"Be a sweetie," Dixie said, fingertips light on his arm. "Buy yourself an air-conditioner like everybody else."

"Tomorrow," Turner finally conceded. "I'll have it down tomorrow."

Dixie smiled. She stowed the ironing-board in her car and left.

That evening Turner drank four beers. He rolled and

smoked cigarette after cigarette. He was grousing and calculating how long he could run the sprinkler before Dixie might be back when his phone rang.

"It sank," his brother said.

"What?"

"The fucking boat sank."

Turner snorted.

"Oh, real funny," Chris went on. "The dry-rotted thing didn't last ten minutes on the lake. My motor's flooded. All my fishing shit.... Fucked."

"Fucked is right."

"Thanks for the sympathy."

"Hey, we gave it a go," Turner smiled.

"I! I gave it a go! And all my stuff...."

Now Turner was outright guffawing into the phone.

"Thanks for nothing," Chris said and hung up.

Turner grinned inside from chest to skull as he drew another beer from the fridge. His gaze came to dwell on the trailer next door. Where that blue boat had leaned. He imagined his brother 200 yards out on the lake and noticing something wasn't right. Novel coldness to his toes, maybe. No, not right at all.

Chris would've sworn a lot. He would've despaired for a faster motor, the shoreline in sight but hardly nearing, the pads of his fingers blanched bloodless, pressed tight on a throttle that would yield no more than that putt-putt-putt, marking time to the rising of the water. He'd likely make it halfway back, maybe gallingly almost there, a sandwich in a baggie floating at his feet. No, his feet up and perched on the centre seat. Not exactly comfortable. Hah.

Turner paced his kitchen, drank beer, ran a splayed hand through his hair and shook his head. If the tackle box was open, a bobber or two might rise out of it and click red and white against the side of the boat. Turner was conjuring what else might've floated in there before his brother had to give it up and swim. He was gazing again toward the neighbour's trailer, and the stir of his mirth grew complicated.

His head still grinned, but each inbreath stirred more and more disquiet into his chest. A thickening poignancy. He laughed aloud, but he'd had to force matters and no purge came of it.

How that man must have loved his boat. How he must have found solace in the building of it. The floating of it. Solace from turmoil within him? Beyond him? Tasks of family providence gone barren in their everyday? An insurance man? A printer? Or did he cherish his work and was just laid off?

Wherefrom the certainty all of a sudden that Turner should move back to town? The prompt to call his Mom and say hi? And that poor, sad woman with the oblong face. And those kids.... What might it be like, Turner wondered, to raise one of his own? And where had that family gone to now? Downspiralling without the boat.

Four Days from Oregon
Madeleine Thien

I

Once, in the middle of the night, our mother Irene sat on our bed and listed off the ways she was unhappy. She looked out the window and stroked our hair and sometimes she lapsed into silence, as if even she didn't know the full extent of it, where to finish, when to hold back. And all the things that made her unhappy were mixed in with things that made her happy, too, like this house. It was full to the brim. Sometimes, she said, she sat in the bathroom because it was the smallest room with a door that locked. But even then she could hear us all, me and my sisters, Dorrie and Joanne, and our father, all of us creaking the floorboards and talking over the television and stopping up the quiet. Hearing us pulled her out every time. She would come out of the bathroom and chase us down. She said she wanted to pick us up, tuck us under her arm like a rolled-up paper and run away.

We were just kids then, Dorrie was nine, Joanne was seven, and I was six. But we thought of our mother as a little girl; she cried so much and had a temper. She joked about running off on her thirtieth birthday. "Almost there," she told us, laughing, "pack your bags."

When our mother was unhappy, she broke things. She slammed the kitchen door over and over until the window crumpled and fell to the floor. In our bare feet, we tip-toed around the pieces. Our father ignored it. He said, "Tell your crazy mother there's a phone call for her." He said *crazy* with a funny look in his eye, like he didn't really believe it. But we saw it ourselves, the plates flying off her hands in slow time, her face asleep like it was dreaming. Sometimes she broke down and cried, her hands waving in front of her face. Our father turned away and left the house. He walked slowly down the alley.

Irene left us once. She took some clothes and money and went away. We waited for her tirelessly. We woke up in the middle of the night, in our bed wider than a boat, and listened hard. We fought sleep. One day after school, she was back on the couch, her fingers ragged from worry. She'd been crying the whole time. "I missed you," she said, pulling us in. Her black hair swung around and wrapped us in a dark cave. She was crying and laughing. While she was gone, our father had sat at the kitchen table like an old man. He was the same age as our mother, but already his hair had tufts of grey and his skin hung loose around his mouth and eyes. "Like a dog," he said, running his hands over his head, "don't I look just like a dog?"

My sisters and I rode our bikes up and down the alley. When we were winded, we played in the garage, climbing up onto the roof of our father's green Buick. He poked his head in, said, "What's this, now?"

"Tea party," we told him, though we weren't really doing anything at all.

He nodded, "You like it better in the garage than in the house. It's your mother. There's something wrong in her head."

Sometimes Irene was well and she put on the Nutcracker Suite, waltzing us around the room. At times like this, she would gather our father in her arms, gleeful and mournful. She would kiss his face, his eyebrows and mouth, deliberately. He leaned into it, let it happen. He said, "It's not the end of the world." Our mother shook her head gently. "No," she told him, "it never is."

The first time Tom came by, he shook our hands, a big silly grin on his face. He said, "So you're the Terrible Threesome," winking at us. Irene told us he was someone she worked with in the department store. He worked in Sports and Leisure. The second time he came, he brought three badminton rackets and a container full of plastic birdies. We stood in the yard, swung the rackets high above our heads and the birdies clung to the wind and drifted off into the neighbour's yard.

Irene and Tom sat on the back porch drinking pink-tinted coolers. We took turns taking rides on the tire swing our father had tied up with yellow rope. Afterwards, we went down under the porch and filled the concrete blocks with mud. Through the floorboards we could hear Irene's voice, shy and laughing, and the long gaps of silence that came and went all afternoon. We watched Tom drive away. The screendoor swung open then closed, crying out like it needed oil.

Our father came home at six o'clock. Irene locked herself in the bathroom. We said the screendoor needed oiling again and our father took us out back, oil on his hands, and he rubbed it down along the old metal spoke. So when he threw the door open again it closed slow as ever, not a sound on the wind, just the gentle click of the latch closing.

We sat outside with him, our bare legs dangling between the porch steps, our dresses spread like tablecloths. Once, our father showed us an old black-and-white picture, our street a hundred years ago. No cars. Wide streets but no concrete, just the slow movement of day, arcing around then coming back. Women in long dresses bringing up the dust. I told my father I couldn't imagine streets without cars, trolleys coming by and coming by, horses idling on the corners. He said, "It's progress, you see, and it comes whether you welcome it or not."

Sometimes our father had the look of blindness. He said

he could stand on our back steps and look out until the yard disappeared. He saw the house where he grew up, plain as day. It was in another country, and he remembered fields layered into the hillside. A person could grow anything: tea, rice, coffee beans. We remembered this for a long time because he never talked about these things. When he was young, he wanted to be a priest. But he came to Canada and fell in love with our mother.

At night, we can hear them talking, a hushing in the rooms. It's all upside-down. We fall asleep listening to our father crying, Irene's voice lapping overtop. In the mornings they wander out exhausted, our father drifting out the front door, Irene lost in the kitchen.

We spent the entire summer prone in the yard. Dorrie would grab the tire swing and hurl it loose. We lay flat and let it fall toward us, watching it the whole way, the rubber-smell fleeting and then blue sky.

We were there when Irene came running out in her bare feet and our father drove up onto the lawn in the middle of the day. She pulled us up and we ran inside. I cried because I thought the sky was falling. Irene locked us in the bedroom with her.

Our father came up the stairs and banged his fist on the door. "Irene," he said, "open the door."

Irene shook her head. She looked at us and said softly, "Tom will be here soon."

Dorrie went and stood beside her. "How come?"

"Irene!" Our father slammed the door with his fist. "Be reasonable!"

Irene started to cry. We noticed her luggage lined up beside the bed, we were standing right beside it. Three plastic-shell suitcases, pale green. Dorrie started crying, "What's happening, Mom?" Irene unlocked the door and opened it and our father burst inside, his arms swinging. He was still in work clothes, scratchy pants and a white-collared shirt. He was raging at Irene, saying, "I know, I knew it all along. You think I didn't know?" He drove his fist into the closet door and the wood splintered. He turned around and grabbed the curtains and pulled them off the rod and the fabric balled up on the ground. Then he sunk down, too, raging and crying. "Do you know what I've put up with?" he asked. "Everything you do. All your crazy talk. Is this what I deserve?"

Everything was upside-down. Irene froze and stared at him. We heard Tom pull up in the driveway, the thunk of his car door slamming. The sound of the front door and Tom coming all the way up the stairs, we listened to him and waited for him and then he was there, not daring to wink at us again. His blond hair was feathery, lifting away from his face. He held his back straight and came into the room.

I thought my father would stand up, come at him, splinter his face the way he'd splintered the closet. He would tell Irene that enough was enough. But my father got to his feet, his face slick with sweat. He walked toward us, Dorrie and Joanne and me, his mouth collapsing and folding up. He crouched down to touch us and kiss us but we all backed away from him. I started crying. Something about him was repulsive, his tears mixed in with his sweat and his body bending forward like it was broken. He looked at me, disappointed, then he stepped away from us and said to Irene, "Go wherever the hell you want." He never even looked at Tom.

Irene went to the window and watched him walk away down the back steps, walk across the lawn to the car. She was afraid, too. She screamed down at him to get out, even though he was leaving anyway. She went over to the desk, picked up a stack of papers, old bills, letters, and flung them out the window. They showered the lawn. She kept screaming for him to get out, get out, even while he was reversing the car. She pulled his clothes from the closet, shirts and pants tangled together and threw them after him. Tom came and put his arms around her but she pushed away from him.

She started packing, crazy packing, taking our T-shirts and sneakers and hotdogs from the freezer and putting them in one suitcase. Tom had to do everything all over again. Later on, Tom made her lie down and he covered her up with a blanket. He packed our toys, our toothbrushes, our clothes and books. We sat listlessly, leaning against the garage wall. Later they came out and sat on the back steps. It was evening and we could smell the neighbourhood barbecues, burnt sticky haze on the air. Irene said to Tom, "I don't love him anymore." Her voice carried across the yard to where we sat. She stood up and called for us. The wind blew her hair all tangled. "Come inside," she said, her voice shaky.

That night, we climbed into Tom's car, all our bags heavy on top of us. Through the window we saw city collapse into country, concrete sliding into farmhouses, horses looking out into the road. Irene bought ferry tickets like we were a family and we said nothing, let the big rudder push us away from land, the surface water blowing up then skidding back. We rolled off the ferry onto new land, things we'd never seen before, mountains rising up through the middle and ocean on the other side. I thought of my father and the wide wide house, night turning to day and my father moving from room to room, the house creaking gently in the summer heat, crying out because we had left him.

2

Tom started calling us Triple Trouble. He and Irene took us camping on Long Beach, on the very west coast of Vancouver Island. "Quiet time," he said, turning to look at us in the back seat, "so we can sort things out."

Irene was leaving our father because she was in love with Tom. Our mother, who had the face of a girl, told us how she married our father when she was nineteen. He was a good man, she said. He loved Irene very much and she had loved him. But now she was 30, and he was 30, and they had changed. She wanted to do what was best for us. There was no-one to blame. Everything would be okay. Irene started crying then. Tom drove straight ahead. And all the way up into the island mountains, Irene sobbed in the front seat, her chest folding in half. On a winding road, Tom had to pull over and Irene jammed her body out the passenger door, leaned over and threw up on the curb.

My sisters, Dorrie and Joanne, stared silently out the windows. I sat bunched up between them. They were beautiful with shoulder-length black hair and straight cut bangs. Dorrie was the oldest. She bit her lips until they chapped and she chewed her fingernails raw. She was forever picking at herself, pulling loose bits of skin from the corners of her mouth, from her elbows and cuticles. Irene always said to let her be, she'd grow out of it one day. In the car, Dorrie picked at her fingers until they bled so Joanne and I took hold of them. Joanne was crying silently so Dorrie didn't smack us away. She said, "*Do*-on't," but she let us do it.

It was past midnight when we got to Long Beach. Tom drove right up on the sand and parked the car. We couldn't see anything but the moon and the stars. The water was blacked out but we could hear it, a terrible raging. Tom explained about the moon and gravity, how the tides were pulled in, pulled out. "Tomorrow morning, for instance, the tide will come in. Now it's out, so it's safe for us to be here," he laughed, catching our eyes. We were worn out. Dorrie put her arm around me and Joanne laid her head on my lap. He smiled, all his teeth showing. "Oh, I see," he said. "I can see what it's going to be like. You girls are a team right? *Triple Trouble.*" He laughed out loud. Irene stretched her arm out and touched his hair. He beamed at her and she said, "No. Not now. It's too late for jokes."

When we drove to the campsite, the car was silent. Tom got out of the car by himself and started unloading the trunk. There was a big orange tent with metal poles that he put up while Irene held a flashlight steady. He even built a fire, tramping off into the dark and returning with an armload of wood. We fell asleep and Irene woke us, half-dragging and half-carrying us inside and tucking us into sleeping blankets. We slept side-by-side all in a row: Tom, then Irene, then Dorrie, Joanne and me, squished tight in Tom's three-person tent. He left the fire burning, shadow and light playing tricks, slowly wearing out as the night wore on.

We hated them so much it hurt. Dorrie kept a journal and she wrote: *Irene is not our real mother. Our real mother is living with our real father and we've been kidnapped by these hooligans. When the time is right, my sisters and I will run away.* Tom shook his head at us, said, "Where've you been? I was going to take you swimming." He showed us how to crouch down on our hands and knees and blow the fire so smoke rose thick on the air. After dinner, Irene washed our hair under the cold water tap, her fingers rubbing circles. She told us to go and dry by the fire and we stumbled away. Tom poked at the embers with a tree branch.

"How long will we stay here?" Dorrie asked.

Tom shrugged, "Who knows?"

"You shouldn't have brought us, then."

Irene stood behind us with her hands on her hips. "No," she said. "But it was either that or leave you altogether." Joanne started crying again and Irene looked away, embarrassed.

She pulled off her sandals and sat down cross-legged on the ground. She held out her arms for us and we came to

108

her, hesitating, but she crowded us into her lap. Our mother smelled of woodsmoke and outdoors. "It's only temporary," she said, kissing our hair. "Just to see. We'll wait a few days and then go home."

Tom said, "Wait a second, Irene—" and she snapped, "They're my kids. They're mine, okay? I just want to wait and see." Tom leaned toward us and touched her face with the thumbs of his hands. He left sand marks on her, smudges of dirt around her eyes. Irene held us tighter and shook her head. We wanted to run at him, stop thinking and push him down, fill his mouth with sand, push it up his nose until he stopped breathing. Tom turned back to the fire, sweeping up a gust of embers into the black sky.

We sat on logs, tilting our faces to the fire until the heat burned us back. Irene put her arms around our shoulders and squeezed us all tight. We resisted at first but then the smell of her seeped into our noses, and her hair swung around and wrapped us in a dark cave. We held on to her too, our six hands grasping her wrists, her arms, anything we could reach. Until between us there was a silent tussle, holding on so tight our bodies hurt.

The next day, Irene said we had to go on a picnic. They took us to an outcrop of big black rocks where the tide washed up in twenty-foot breakers.

Right away, Tom picked up Irene's hand and said, "Let's go further out." They climbed down on the rocks. We ate potato salad and watched their bodies fold and unfold, Tom's t-shirt flapping in the wind and Irene holding her hair back from her face. In front of them the water burst loud, high as a house ceiling. He lifted her up and she hooked her arms around his neck. If he let go, she would just hang there, her body swinging back and forth.

Joanne picked up the big glass bowl of potato salad. "Watch me," she said, and flung it between the rocks. The bowl broke and the potato salad fell out in a big lump. She shrieked with laughter. "Take these," she ordered, handing me Tom's sunglasses and Irene's brown sandals. Joanne swung the two-litre bottle of orange pop through the air like a baseball bat. We watched it go, it bounced twice and sprung a leak, washing up in the shallow pool

Dorrie leaned her body over the rocks. "Goodbye," she laughed, "*good*-bye."

"For Chrissake," Tom yelled, "for Christ's fucking sake." He grabbed his sunglasses out of my hands. Shaking his head, he picked up what was left then pushed past us to the gravel parking-lot.

"For *Christ's fucking sake*," Joanne laughed.

Irene stood looking at us. There were drops of water on her skin and the sun caught on them and made them glitter. She started to move closer but we stared her down, stared so hard she stopped walking, brushed her foot in the dirt and drew a line. Her voice was low, "You don't believe me now, but it's better like this." She nodded her head. "I know you think it couldn't be. You think nothing is worse than this. But believe me, there are worse things." I was still holding her brown sandals. When I dropped them, they skidded down the rocks and fell without splashing into the water below. Irene said, "Gail," and shook her head. She turned away from us, walked back to the road in her bare feet.

I dreamed I could see nothing. Off the rocks and onto the gravel, I heard nothing, not Tom or Irene or the wind shaking the windows or the rain starting to fall. We climbed into the car and Tom pulled roughly away from the parking-lot. I closed my eyes and dreamed of a wide, wide space we could tumble through silent and together. The car idled at intersections, hit highway and went fast and smooth.

Tom said, "This is what I think. I think we should leave tomorrow. You don't think he'll follow us, right? You said so yourself, he doesn't care. Four days is long enough. If he doesn't care, let's just go."

Our bodies fell together as if the car was tipping, one body slumped to the next. Irene bowed her head, "Yes," she nodded, "let's leave tomorrow."

"Where?" I asked.

Tom said, "To stay with my sister. She has a cottage, right beside the ocean, just like here."

Irene turned around to face us, her face wrecked. "Tom and I will take care of everything. When it's warm you can swim in the ocean. I'm going to get a job, in a store maybe. You'll meet all new kids."

Dorrie shook her head. "We already have friends."

"New kids," Irene said, smiling stubbornly. "You'll make new friends."

"We don't want new friends or a new school," Joanne said. "You said we'd go back. You promised. You said we'd stay here a few days and then go home."

Tom cut in, "Look, it isn't easy for any of us."

"I don't know," Irene shook her head.

Dorrie was crying, "How come you can't keep your promises?"

She said, "Don't talk to me that way."

"You lied to us, you said we'd go home."

"I didn't say that. I said maybe. Maybe isn't the same thing. And anyway it's too late to go back now."

"Why?"

"Because I've decided, okay? I've decided to go, we're going and that's all." She turned around in her seat.

"You never asked us," Joanne said.

"Maybe we would have stayed with him," I whispered. "Maybe we wouldn't have missed you. I miss him, maybe we wouldn't have missed you."

Irene didn't move. "No," she nodded, her voice soft, "I wasn't thinking about you."

Tom put one arm around her. She leaned toward him and then she half turned and her face was against his sleeve. We were waiting for her to lash out, to bang her fist against the window or throw something, smash the cassette tapes on the floor. But she stayed where she was, he patted her shoulder slow and steady and she never moved.

The car hit 80, 90, 120 and Tom looked sideways at Irene. He was nothing like our father. Tom's face was handsome and strong, light blond hair that curled in tufts. Our father's face was dark and sad. Our father combed his hair with Brylcreem until it shone. He smelled of eucalyptus and cooking and warmth. But he and Tom looked at Irene with the same face, mixed-up sadness and love and strange devotion.

That night, we listened to them breathing, the heaviness of it like their bodies were emptying out. We listened for animals, for a bear to come crashing through the trees. It could hear that breathing, we thought, and it would be drawn to us.

They said words aloud, mumbled liked they were whispering secrets. She said, "Tom," and he started awake, put his arm around her.

Our stomachs hurt. We pressed them gingerly, wondered aloud if we had cancer, or if we were dying, slowly, in the middle of the woods and no-one around. We heard other campers walking by, the finger probe of their flashlights sliding across the tent, the trudge-trudge of their feet on gravel.

Still Irene and Tom slept. Even when the ocean sounded so loud it seemed like it was coming to us, all the land pushed under like a broken bowl, they slept breathing heavily. We fell in and out of dreams, finally waking hours after they had risen. Tom slid the metal poles smoothly through the loops and the tent came down, the orange fabric floating like a full moon toward us.

3

They had their first argument our first night in Oregon. Tom's sister watched silently, standing in the doorway. We ran outside and stood on the front lawn in our bare feet, the sky wider than we had ever known it, so much salt on the air. We could hear Irene from the street. She screamed that he had tricked her, he had made her come here, what would she do now, she was lost. Tom's voice was muffled in the background. "Irene," he said, "please, Irene." We sat on the curb and when she ran out to us she was sobbing. "Shhh," Dorrie said, petting her back, "shh-shhh." Irene leaned her head against us. "We'll go back," she whispered. "Okay? We'll go back." In the morning we woke up and found Tom and Irene sprawled together on the basement couch, their arms and legs all tangled up, Irene's hair sliding across Tom's face.

It was easy to love Gentle Bend. Every day, we strolled along the boulevard, past the ice cream shops and the fish & chip stands. Mothers in bikinis towed their children behind them. In the ocean, they were neon bobs floating on the surface, their water wings dancing. "Every summer is the same here," Tom told us. "It never changes."

He took us walking on the shoreline, white tufts of foam gathering at our feet and the moon hanging low. He said, "Irene will be okay. Just give her time." We sat down on the sand and I saw the moon tugging the ocean in, dragging it in on its belly. I imagined it would lay itself down on us like a blanket then all of us would ride out to sea, our nightgowns trailing out like the sails of a boat. In the day we would sink down to the surface, walk on the water's floor, stand still and close our eyes while the fish brushed by, skin to skin. Faraway a voice would be calling us home, but through the water that voice would disintegrate and break into light and we would walk past, not noticing.

113

There was a time in Gentle Bend when I couldn't get away fast enough. It is a Sleeping Beauty town, waking up in the summer kissed by tourists. Music on the bandstand and everyone snapping pictures of the 60-foot frying pan that stands beside the town office (it stands upright, wooden handle pointing to the sky). It was given as a gift to the city in 1919, a tribute to the women who remained behind during the First World War. It is the world's largest. The night we got here, Tom ushered us all up to it and we sat down on the lip. Irene watched from the car while Tom snapped a Polaroid. I was looking past him, to Irene's face framed in the passenger window, her hair blowing out beside her. "How do you like it?" Tom asked, beaming. "I hate it," I said spitefully.

Tom's face fell. "Why?" he asked. "Everyone wants to live at the seaside."

Come fall, the tourists disappeared and half the shops boarded up for the off-season. Then Dorrie and Joanne and I walked along the beach, the sky overcast, the horizon dense with mist. Dorrie bit her lips and creased her brow, always troubled and anxious. Joanne sprinted in front of us, kicking at the tufts of foam and sending them through the air like cotton, yelling aloud about all the things she would do when she left Gentle Bend. "I'm going to be a trucker!" she said once, her voice catching in the tides. "And never stay put."

When she was nineteen, Dorrie got married and moved to Vancouver. That same year, Joanne packed her bags and left, caught a bus and then a ferry to Victoria. Late one night she had cried her heart out to Tom and he had given her the money to leave. "She'll be okay," he told Irene that morning, his eyes puffy. They sat at the kitchen table for hours and in the afternoon they lay down together and fell into a heavy sleep.

I believe I am the only one who never loved Tom. Eventually, Dorrie and Joanne learned. They went to him instead of Irene. They told him about their boyfriends and their problems, the girls in school, the nights they crept out of the house and slept on the beach. They saw his sympathy, I think. When Irene had her breakdowns, they saw how he held her, how he comforted her and didn't let go until she was well again.

I yearned for my father. Even though he had never been any of these things, I yearned for him. I wanted the man who I resembled, whose nose and eyes I had inherited, who had given me what—I'd never know. Sometimes at night, Irene and I would sit in the kitchen and listen to the three of them talking outside. She read books or magazines, *Good Housekeeping* or *Woman's World*, but mostly she stared into space. Irene aged well. Sometimes now, I think she looks younger than my sisters or I. When she was at her worst, when I felt forced to run outside (on the driveway still I could hear glass breaking, pots thrown against the wall) her face was calm, beautiful even.

I tried to get her to talk about our father. But she would shake her head, say, "Why do you ask me these things?" Once she asked me if I was trying, really trying to make her crazy, and another time, if I hated her still, if I still had not forgiven her. "Why can't you let it go?" she asked me, pushing the dishes under the soapy water, bubbles on her cheek where she had laid her fingers.

I always meant to find my father. All the time, people do it. In this century, nobody can stay lost unless you let them. Years ago, my sisters and I watched a magician on TV make the Statue of Liberty disappear. Our father turned around and said, "Smoke and mirrors. Nothing can disappear just like that," and we believed him, even though we had seen it with our own eyes. But then gaps of time would go by and I never did anything with them. And it isn't like standing still. If you ignore the thing you want long enough, it begins to recede. You get older and nothing is clear.

I got a job with the town, giving walking tours during

the summers to tourists. Taking them along the boulevard, past the wax museum and the spaghetti shop. To the frying pan where everyone gathered around me and I told the long story, thinking they'd repeat it sometime, musing on it, laughing at why we need our memories so big.

Tom and Irene own a sporting-goods store in Gentle Bend, selling things like scuba gear, flippers and surf boards. In the mornings, Tom takes a walk inland, just for the pleasure of turning around again and walking downhill to the ocean. Irene stands at the front of the steps looking out for him, her face young as it ever was, her dark hair folded on her shoulders. She has a longing for him. I could be standing right beside her and she wouldn't even know me. Like back when we were camping on Vancouver Island. She would crawl into the tent after Tom and we would sit around the campfire while it burned down, scratching at the dirt with our feet to let her know that we were still there.

I am 25 years old and I don't know if I will ever leave this town. One day I would like to go inland, just to see what it might have been like. But I want to come back here, watch the slowest change we could ever see, my parents ageing, the beach washing back from the water. Sometimes I know what I have inherited from my father. We are the ones who stay behind. We see the others come and go, and when they leave we do not stop them and we pretend we will not miss them. We wait, see our lives and our homes change, come apart, and change again. Maybe when I am 60, the town itself will have receded. All of us who stay here will creep backwards too, watching and watching for change, then being surprised when it strikes us, out of the blue, no reason but the fact that it is all different, it must be. Irene and Tom and I sit in the kitchen reading books and magazines, from morning till night we can hear the water and the wind and two mixing together and the fire hushing, hushing in our little room.

Balinese

Adam Lewis Schroeder

The dirt road was red and dusty, undulating gently with the landscape. Every now and then a stone shrine stood idly by the roadside, three or four feet high and tapering into a point, decorated around its base with orange and yellow blossoms, sticks of pungent incense and bowls filled with rice. Insects droned over the offerings. Tall palms waved above the road, and on either side terraced rice padis clambered one on top of the other as far as the eye could see.

Potgieter went up the road carrying his suitcase in his left hand, his starched shirt riding uncomfortably across his hot shoulders. He hummed a song.

Oh, give me land lots of land under starry skies above,
Don't fence me in.

On the ship from Holland a band in white dinner jackets had played this American song. They'd just come out of the Red Sea into the Gulf of Aden, and at that moment it seemed a fitting theme for adventure of any variety.

He no longer paid the little shrines much attention, he'd already seen so many in the eight miles he'd walked. But they seemed to be increasing in frequency as he walked along and yes, certainly that had to be a rooftop behind those trees, yes now he was nearing the village.

The boat from Holland had only gone as far as Batavia, on Java. The colonial authorities had been very civilized, and had come to his hotel in order to inquire into his further plans in the Dutch East Indies. Was he interested in the colonial service? A plantation? Or was he a missionary? "No, no," he had answered, and the one man had suddenly looked up from the form he'd been filling out and the other had set down his drink, "No, you see I am a painter. I have seen some photographs of this place Bali and I will go there to paint. I think it is a lovely place."

"And the women there," the one with the drink had said. "Lord, Lord, the women."

In the padi to the left of the road a line of people suddenly stood up and stretched themselves, and Potgieter felt his eyebrows rise up in surprise, setting creases in the shimmering-sweaty skin of his forehead. Young men and women dressed in sarongs and broad hats, stretching their hands high above their heads in the middle of the bright padi, some waving tiny scythes with remnants of weed clinging to them. Their bare torsos orangey-brown and smudged with dirt, the skin of the breasts taut, the muscles deeply drawn and sinewy. They smiled at one another, chattering, then finally they brought their arms down and started single-file along the stone edge of the terrace. Potgieter realized then that he had stopped walking. A shout went up in the padi.

The Balinese came bounding onto the road, spilling all around him, the four or five young men instantly in a circle, touching his shoulders and up and down his arms, smiling, their dark lashes slowly flickering. They were all the same height and Potgieter ten inches taller than that. He smiled broadly at them, nodding his head from one man to the next and then to the women waiting beneath the coconut palm, saying to himself, I'm not scared, I have no reason to be scared, I'm not. Then the men started pointing up the road, the way he was going, and Potgieter nodded vaguely, so one of the men took his suitcase from his hand and another started shuffling up the road in a sort of dance, hooting like a monkey and kicking up the dust.

"Hanuman," said one of the women. She laced an arm around the bare waist of her companion and the whole party started up the road.

Potgieter sat at his easel. His suitcase had held only canvases, brushes and paint—the largest tins available from Coenraad's Art Supply of Rotterdam—so he'd had no European clothes to change into when his suit had become too soiled to wear. When the fat woman had collected the filthy clothes for washing she'd left him a long green sarong to wear in their stead, but he hadn't known how to properly wear it, folding it down snugly over the hips, so he'd fastened the fabric to him with his leather belt. The fat woman had laughed and laughed, so hard that she'd started to lose her breath, and stood fluttering her hands in the air like birds.

He lived in a wooden house just outside the stone walls of the fat woman's family compound. She was the only fat woman in the village, and Potgieter thought it likely, from what little of the island he had seen, that she was the only fat woman on Bali. She had a young daughter about twelve whose breasts were beginning to grow, a lovely little thing called Jata. Two of her front teeth were rotten and brown. Often the fat woman would set the daughter to work beside the path in front of Potgieter's house, weaving a mat or picking the weevils from a basket of rice. Potgieter assumed the reason the fat woman didn't ask him to pay rent was that she expected him to marry Jata before long. So as he leapt off his porch each morning, ready to see what was new in the village, who he might meet, what he might paint, what sort of fruit might be for sale in the little market, he would quickly say hello to her.

"Good morning," he'd say in Balinese. It was one of his few phrases.

"Good morning sir," she'd say, her eyes on her work. "Do you go to work in the rice padi?"

"I'm sorry," he'd say in Dutch, "I don't understand what you're saying."

So she would keep her eyes on her work.

Potgieter sat in a sarong at his easel, painting a picture of Dalem, the young man who had carried his suitcase. They were beside the village's north temple. Its high walls, carved with monkeys and grimacing demons, surrounded a deserted gravel courtyard and a long row of elegant shrines, each spiked with lazy-burning sticks of incense set out that morning by women on their way to the fields.

Dalem stood leaning in the arched doorway, his sarong hanging loosely off his hips, his arms folded. With great precision and patience Potgieter was committing every detail, of the wall, of the steps, of the sarong, of Dalem's face, his fingers, chest, feet, to the canvas. He tried to suggest a sort of glow emanating from behind Dalem's figure with a pale yellow wash, so thin he brushed it on three times and still wasn't sure if it was visible. Then he decided that the artificial glow wasn't necessary, that the most he could do to convey his feeling toward the place, the wonder, the somehow magical newness of it all, was to portray things just as they were. Why should I try to make it shining and new, he thought, when really it is so ancient? The most evocative picture of the place would show exactly what he saw.

He put his brush down and took a cigarette out of the packet in his paint-box. As he lit it Dalem came down out of the doorway, and took the second drag from the cigarette once Potgieter had had the first.

"Dalem!" came a voice from around the corner of the temple, and Dalem's father, Nyoman, came striding after it, a short thick man with a thatch of black hair piled high atop his head. Dalem quickly handed the cigarette back to Potgieter.

"Good afternoon," Potgieter called out, in his best Balinese.

Nyoman pretended that Potgieter was not there. He hurried up, took Dalem by the wrist and led him away.

"What's going on?" said Dalem.

"Your brother is in trouble, I need your help," said Nyoman.

Dalem had tried to explain to Potgieter, a few days before, that he had a brother who was crazy and was always pissing on things.

Nyoman pulled his son up the path, and though Dalem struggled to pull his wrist free, his father was very powerful.

Potgieter sat waving goodbye.

When Potgieter was in Batavia his friends from the colonial government had unrolled a map of Bali on their table in the hotel bar, and he'd selected his village by taking his eyes away and putting his finger down on the map. Unfortunately the place sat isolated at the foot of the mountains, many miles inland. No traffic went through it and he'd never be able to hire a boat to ferry him anywhere.

"We'll have some trouble keeping tabs on you out there," the one with the pile of forms had said. "We'll have you report in once a month for a start and see if you need any help."

"If you can come up for air," the one with the drink had said, and he gave a long whistle.

So after one month in the village Potgieter had to return to Denpasar, the capital of the island, to report to the authorities on his artistic progress. He had trained in Holland as a cartographer, and he wondered whether, if he was not producing paintings of a minimum quality, he might be set to work mapping the more recent of the Dutch acquisitions in the Indies: the Bird's Head Peninsula, Tanimbar, Aceh, names as exotic as Bali itself. But no, his village was where he wanted to stay, and with determination he rolled his canvases under his arm and started down the road.

He walked for hours, always trying to keep south, finally

seeing people on the road somewhere near Ubud and getting a ride on a bullock cart just east of there. The back of the cart was filled with pieces of sculpture of various shapes and sizes, bound for repairs in Batubulan, the stone-carving town, and the driver kept turning in his seat to point the beauty of the various pieces out to him, but Potgieter didn't pay any attention. He had never had much of an eye for sculpture.

On the road out of Batubulan, once more on foot, Potgieter heard an automobile approaching from behind him and turned to wave it down. By an amazing coincidence the car contained two Dutch civil servants on their way to Denpasar.

"We're going to the Stadthaus," said the bald one. "Will that be all right?"

"That is the place I want to go," said Potgieter.

"I see," said the one with the pipe, who was driving. "You want to go home."

"Home to my village, yes. North of Ubud."

"Do you have a plantation? I didn't think that a plantation on Bali could be worthwhile," said the driver. "Nobody can grow rice like these Balinese. You can't beat them."

"I'm a painter," said Potgieter.

"Housepainter?" said the bald one.

At the Stadthaus, Potgieter was sent to an upstairs room where two men and a woman were waiting for him. The woman was there because she was the wife of one of the district officers, and considered to be very artistic. Potgieter unrolled his canvases on the long table and the men weighed down the ends with heavy books.

"Don't you like the Expressionists?" said the woman. "It doesn't seem that you do."

"This buffalo has such long eyelashes. Were they really that long?" said one of the men.

"That was the reason for me to pick that buffalo," said Potgieter.

"The buffalo is good," said the woman.

"I like this boy," said the second man. It was the painting of Dalem. Everyone came over to look.

"I hope you won't take offence at my asking, but being a fellow artist I'll assume you won't mind," said the woman. Everyone looked over at her. "Are you homosexual, Mr. Potgieter?"

"No," said Potgieter.

"Looking at this picture I'd say you were," she said.

"That's the sort of thing the Japanese wouldn't appreciate," said the first man, tipping his head toward the picture.

"Here we go," said the second.

"What do you mean?" said Potgieter.

"The Japanese aren't nearly as open toward the idea of homosexuality as we Dutch."

"What do you mean we're open to it? In the courts it's a felony," said the second man.

"I'd heard just the opposite about the Japanese," said the woman. "I'd heard that the officers all slept in one another's beds."

"Oh really?" said the first man. "Well in the army I suppose it's all the same, no matter where you're from."

"Why is this, that we discuss Japan?" said Potgieter.

"You know," said the second man, "Manchuria, Korea, Indo-China...."

"They seem to be headed this way," said the woman. "To put it bluntly."

"And they will be here soon?" said Potgieter.

"Oh, maybe never," said the first man, "maybe in a year or two. Still, it's something to think about." He waved a hand blandly at Potgieter, and put on his hat.

"I like the paintings," said the second man.

"We'll send them back to Holland for a show," said the first man. "Just leave them there. Come on, I have to get to my lunch."

"Yes, I'll have to meet my husband soon," said the

woman, looking down at her tiny wrist-watch.

"Listen, Mr. Potgieter, do you need paints and things?" said the second man. "Because the picture of that young man really is excellent."

"Listen to you," said the first man.

Dalem was not working in the padi any more. The women came by to ask if he would pitch in, they were in the middle of harvest and his experienced hands would be useful. But Dalem said no, Potgieter needed his help. One of the girls asked if Potgieter wanted to paint her again, but Dalem said no, he probably didn't. And at last the women went away.

Dalem went back into Potgieter's house, shut the door behind him and quickly undid his sarong. The hair around his privates was fine and downy. He sat in a chair beside the window, pulled his legs slightly apart, tilted his head back, the light falling across him.

"Good," said Potgieter. He sat at his easel, in the opposite corner of the room. The canvas was more or less black, dark browns, with Dalem's figure and the shape of the window painted in brilliant whites and blues and yellows in the centre. The light gleamed across his skin. Potgieter had been tempted to put a pastoral scene in the window, the rice harvest or a buffalo passing, but instead had represented it just as a square of light, keeping the viewer's attention on Dalem.

Potgieter thought of how, two days before, he had bicycled down to Ubud for supplies. The district officer's wife had arranged for a box to be sent up for him each month from Denpasar. He picked the box up at a house in the centre of town, owned by an Englishman, Mr. Ross, who had come to Bali to study gamelan music. Three or four young women always followed Mr. Ross around, and Ross himself always had a flower in his hair. This time the box contained a letter from Holland, from Potgieter's brother.

"Is it more news about the terrible weather, or the ugly women?" said Ross, in English.

Potgieter was not listening, but he nodded and pursed his lips.

Went to your exhibition yesterday evening, hundreds of people there. Ma couldn't believe it. Bali looks like a nice place. Who is the young man? Everyone was asking me as if I ought to know. Ma told everyone he was a prince who had commissioned you to paint a series of portraits and that you'd made a pile. A group of painters say they want to go to Bali now too, to have a look, but at the same time everyone's saying that no-one ought to go anywhere until we see what happens with Herr Hitler. Dad's eyes are as bad as ever, he made Trixie read him the newspaper from start to finish.

Now, as Dalem sat beside the window, Potgieter imagined this very painting on the wall of the Rijksmuseum in Amsterdam, all his teachers, relatives, friends from the army filing past it, some turning away, some whistling. He was homesick for Holland, he wanted to drink some cognac, go to the cinema, hear a band play jazz, eat some potatoes. But he knew that after a few days he'd just become homesick for Bali and it would be worse than any longing he'd ever had for Holland. It had turned out so well here. He thought of himself walking up the dusty road, suitcase in hand, and felt sorry for that Potgieter, who was so unsure of what the future would hold.

Let me ride through the wide open country that I love,
Don't fence me in.

"What's that?" said Dalem.

"Song," said Potgieter, dabbing at the palate.

Dalem gave a broad smile. "What song?"

"American song," said Potgieter.

"America," said Dalem. He had never heard of it.

A few months later Potgieter went to Ubud and Mr. Ross was not at home. The women sat in the courtyard of his house, scraping out coconuts, and the youngest of these ladies spoke English very well.

"Neville returned to England," she said.

"Why?" said Potgieter.

"He had to be with his family at this important time."

"Was someone sick? Did someone die?"

"He want to be in the Royal Air Force," said another of the girls, and they all shaped their hands like airplanes and flew them through the air.

Potgieter collected his box and found a letter from the district officer's wife between the paint cans.

When Mr. Pieterszoon and I heard war had been declared we started packing for home. He resigned his commission here and will try to rejoin his regiment. I hope you have not made any German friends because they will be arrested soon. Trying to get a few letters off while the other passengers are boarding. Hope to see you at home, we live in Enschede, hope you can continue painting.

He realized then that the box of paint would have to last him a long time.

Jata met him on the road back to the village. She looked very pleased, her pink tongue showing through the gap where her front teeth had been.

"Dalem had to go to Padangbai," she said.

"He did? Why?" By this time his Balinese was much better.

"His cousin is there. They say he'd been here long enough and he should learn how to fish and to sail a boat."

Potgieter was looking across the padis to the east, in the direction of Padangbai.

"When did this happen?" he said.

"His uncle came on a horse this morning and Dalem got on the back."

"But I only left this morning!"

"They took him as soon as you had gone." Jata bit her lip. "Do you like horses?"

Potgieter didn't answer. Every time his left pedal descended it let out a shriek. Jata trotted along beside the bicycle. A breeze was blowing and the dirt on the road looked rich and inviting. Potgieter stopped pedalling and when the bicycle came to a stop he put his feet down on the ground.

"Do you want to ride up here?" he said. He tapped the flat of his fingernail against the wide handlebars. Jata climbed up and carefully held her sarong out of the way of the front wheel.

Potgieter's hair had gone very blond after so long in the sun, and his arms and torso were a dark earth-tone. He squatted in the padi, weeding. Thorny little plants grew in the spaces between the tender rice shoots, and he would wind the stalk of each weed around his thick finger and pull, meticulously, one after the other. The irrigation water was up to his ankles. Half a dozen men and women from the village squatted on either side of him, humming to themselves, their hands working away, their arms and faces smeared with dirt. But for his size, his hair, Potgieter looked just as they did.

It had been three years since he first came to the village. He had stopped painting, because he had run out of paint and because Dalem had gone. And he didn't know where his European clothes were, he assumed the fat woman had them somewhere in her house. She had once asked Potgieter if he'd ever been to Batavia because that's where her husband had said he was going, years before.

Potgieter's hands were so leathery, he couldn't feel the thorns from the plants he pulled up. When he'd first entered the army he had sat on his bunk and studied his hands, his poor painter's hands condemned to being soldier's hands, and now hundreds of thoughts like that flowed through his head, his hands kept pulling weeds and his past on Bali and in Holland flickered through his mind's eye, compressing years and people, expanding certain moments to fill an hour. He wished at times that he could sit in a cinema and watch these things sail by on the screen, he'd be able to appreciate then what a beautiful girl she had been, what a sad and tired man the headmaster had been, and hadn't it been a lovely day when he and his father had had that terrible quarrel? He knew that, aesthetically, his life had been one to envy. But in reality he felt only the frustration, the longing, he couldn't escape the bothersome emotion attached to each moment no matter how long past. So the days in the padi were gloomy ones, because of his thoughts.

One day he told the fat woman he was going to ride his bicycle to Padangbai, and soon it seemed the whole village knew, because as he was tying his clothes into a bundle Nyoman came to the door.

"Mr. Potga," he said, "are you going to Padangbai?"

"Yes, I am," said Potgieter, and because he was in high spirits he smiled at the stout little man. "Do you want to come with me?"

"I know you are going to see Dalem," said Nyoman, and suddenly he gave a little bow to Potgieter. "I ask you, for my family, to not go to Padangbai."

Potgieter got up and went over to the door. He towered over Nyoman.

"I only want to say hello to my friend. Dalem is my friend."

Nyoman kept his head lowered.

"I beg you not to do this," he said.

Later on the fat woman brought Potgieter a chicken in a basket. It was from Dalem's mother, to take to her son.

With the basket tied to his bicycle he pedalled down the muddy and rutted road. It was the rainy season. Jata would not come out of the compound to say goodbye. Her mother said to not take it personally, many evil spirits were about that particular day, and an unmarried woman couldn't take any chances. "But I'm not afraid of them," she said, and shook the rolls of her fat stomach with her hands.

It took him a day and a night to reach Padangbai, on the eastern coast. It was a dismal morning when he arrived, and only one fishing boat was on the water. The rest were pulled up on the sand, bright blue or bright yellow, each with the jutting head of a swordfish carved into its bow, their wooden eyes rolled back in their heads toward the sea.

When the boat came in Dalem stepped off into the shallows and trotted up to where Potgieter stood leaning on his bicycle. Potgieter tried not to grin, but he couldn't help it.

"What are you doing here?" said Dalem.

"I have come to say hello. I want to find out if you like it here."

"Well, I like the boats. I don't miss the rice padis, you know. How is my brother, is he the same?"

"I'm afraid he is."

"I don't miss that."

Two other men pulled the boat up onto the sand and walked up to the village, carrying the nets. Potgieter saw them look their direction, heard them mutter the word *husband*.

Dalem was not looking at Potgieter, he was looking out over the water. Potgieter saw that he was more muscular now, his shoulders were broader, but he held himself with the same grace as always.

"You know," said Dalem, "the government will pay a lot of money to anyone who sees a military boat." He swept an arm over the sea. "If I'm lucky I'll see a few of them."

"I hope you can let me know, when you see one."

"Maybe," said Dalem. A small orange crab appeared from behind a rock and made a wide circle around them on its way to the sea. Dalem's eyes skirted over the water, habitually.

"Then maybe," said Potgieter, "you can come and carry me away the same way they carried you away."

Dalem gave a short laugh, looked him briefly in the face,

and Potgieter took hope.

"Maybe you will come back to the village to be painted," he said.

Dalem blew his nose into his hand and threw the mucous down onto the sand.

"You know, I have a bad cold. I should not be travelling."

The chicken clucked a few times from inside the basket, trying to sleep with its head under a wing. Dalem's uncle's family at least would be happy to see Potgieter, as they had not had chicken to eat in some time.

"I don't have any paints left anyway," Potgieter said.

Later he regretted saying it. At work in the rice padi he cursed himself time and again.

Padangbai was a grey and filthy place in his mind's eye, full of diseased dogs and pigs and men with fingers missing, houses falling apart and animal droppings. But maybe that impression was unfair, had been left by the slate-grey sky and the rain while he had been there, had been left by Dalem.

He tugged weeds away from the tender rice shoots.

Jata's cousin Airlan was a stone carver. One day he came to Potgieter's house, in his white shirt and black sarong, tapping two chisels against each other *ting ting ting*.

"Hello, Potga," he said. "I wonder if you know about carving."

"I don't know anything. I used to know about painting, but I can't quite remember."

"Come on now," said Airlan, "you can help me."

They went around to Airlan's compound, behind the fat woman's, through the special gate that evil spirits could not blow through, and knelt down together under a bamboo canopy attached to the main house.

Airlan taught him to shape blocks of stone with a chisel and mallet, and Potgieter worked thick calluses into his hands. It was not so different from painting, he thought, taking something shapeless and making a shape, something people could see as a fragment of their own lives, something that wouldn't have existed at all but for his efforts. They were working on a stone bull to go outside the headman's temple. The muscles through his back and arms ached for the first while, but then they relaxed, and he finally looked at what he'd carved and he realized that the sculpture wasn't going anywhere, any stranger from anywhere could happen upon it, it was a part of the landscape as permanent as a tree or a mountainside. It was what defined everything in Bali, the spirit of the eternal running through everything like a vein of silver. Unlike any frail piece of canvas hanging in the Rijksmuseum.

Someone from another village said that the Japanese had bombed the city of Surabaya, on Java, and that all the citizens had run away. The villagers asked Potgieter how big Surabaya was and how many people did that mean would have run away, and though he had not been there he knew it was a big place, so he pointed out to the rice padi and said that if all the little rice plants as far as you could see got up and ran away that's what it would be like.

"And they're all small like that?" said Jata, beaming.

He had not heard from anyone in Holland for a long time. A Balinese man in Ubud who had worked for the government told him that a peace treaty had been arranged with Germany, but neither of them could guess what that meant. Maybe Holland had claimed some new ground in Germany. Maybe the two armies were fighting in trenches outside Amsterdam, with barbed wire and mustard gas.

But he missed Holland less and less. Whenever he craved veal or beer or potatoes he would remind himself that in Holland he would have to wear a suit and tie and shoes while consuming them. And he would look down at his brown feet with pride.

For months Airlan and Potgieter worked on a huge carving of Hanuman the monkey god, on one of the inside walls of the north temple. There was a large ceremony when it was completed; the priest spent nearly an hour chanting and sprinkling the new carving with holy water, and everyone in the village came to watch. They sat in the courtyard lit with candles.

"Hanuman has always been my favourite," said the fat woman.

"I like Sita," said Jata.

"When you're an old woman you'll like Hanuman better. He's got spark."

"Like you have?" said Jata.

"There's monkey in our family a long way back," said the fat woman.

"Auntie, please don't say that," Airlan said quietly. "There are lots of people here."

"You like monkeys, don't you Potga?" said Jata.

"No," said Potgieter. "Are you the monkey?"

"His teeth aren't big enough," said the headman's wife, pointing at the statue. "I like Hanuman to have great big teeth. Then he bites a chunk out of that demon."

"He kicks," said the fat woman. "He doesn't bite."

Jata took Potgieter's arm as she sat beside him and leaned her head on his shoulder, so that her black hair fell in streams down his white tunic. He took her little hand and she pressed her fingernails lightly into his palm, and he smiled at that.

They were going to be married in a few months' time.

He didn't think about Dalem anymore. He worked with Airlan for long hours, day after day, one sliver of stone chipped away after another, the rock cold and solid under his hand, and sometimes when he was needed he'd go into the padis with Jata, to plant rice, to weed, to harvest. His rolled-up canvases sat up in the rafters of his little house.

One day he saw an old man leading a buffalo down a path, with three or four chickens on the buffalo's back, and after a moment Potgieter realized that the chickens were sitting in his open suitcase, tied to the bull with a rope. There were no handles on the suitcase and it was nearly black, stained with years of chicken droppings. He laughed to himself, but when he told Jata she said it was a terrible way to treat a suitcase that had come all the way from Holland.

He and Airlan took their cart and went to the same place they always did, a cliff at the foot of the mountains, and brought back a slab of grey rock. Potgieter looked at it for a while, contemplating its volume in the space it would occupy, which parts of the stone were meant to stay as they were and which were meant to go. The ideas about colour that he once would have had never even came into his mind. He started carving a shrine in front of his house; the god that would bless his marriage was going to live there. After Potgieter had chipped away the shape Airlan did some delicate work, a tiny monkey on the top, a line of birds around the middle.

"These birds brought you from Holland," said Airlan.

"I came on a huge boat," said Potgieter, and he spread his arms wide.

"I know that," said Airlan.

The priest came and blessed the shrine. The fat woman's family set sticks of incense into the narrow holes Potgieter had carved, and people from the village set fruit and dishes of rice around its base.

"It will be a bountiful marriage," said the priest. Potgieter bowed low. The wedding ceremony was to be in ten days; the date was one of the most auspicious on the calendar.

"You'll be a pretty husband," said Jata.

He nodded his head gratefully to everyone around them, but did not look at Jata.

It was four days later, a hot morning, bright and green, when the Japanese came up the road. Potgieter and Jata and a few others were in the padi some distance from the village, kneeling in the soft mud, when his eye caught a spark, a movement, and he lifted his eyes from the rice plants to look. It was sunlight glinting off a bayonet. There were six soldiers on the road marching ahead of a jeep, all moving silently, almost beautifully, gliding beneath the coconut palms.

"They must be on their way somewhere," said Jata. Then she held her lips tight together but Potgieter saw how frightened she was. And he knew, had known since leaving Batavia, that the road went only to their village and no farther.

The Japanese went nearer and nearer the village, the broad leaves of the palms rustling softly over their heads, a mist of red dust rising and patiently falling in their wake. The soldiers moved behind the first house and disappeared from sight. Everything was silent. A dog barked in the village, once.

Potgieter stood up, his feet sinking into the padi a little. The sun was already hot over their heads. He felt a little nauseated, and wiped his weak hands on his sarong, smearing the fabric with dark mud. He imagined the fat woman running from her family compound, waving her arms, saying, "I know where the Dutchman is! I'll take you to him! Come with me! To the Dutchman!" And the Japanese following her. But no, he thought, it wouldn't be her, it would be Nyoman.

Potgieter wiped his wet hands again and began to walk across the padi to the village. Jata stood up. "I'll see what they want," he said. Jata did not follow him and the others went on working.

He stepped onto the road and a small boy came running up to him from the village, followed by two more boys and a little girl, all with triumphant grins. When they reached him the children took his hands and began to drag him along, his feet bumping along in the dust as he went along with them.

"Japan," said one of the boys.

"Japan," said the second, nodding.

"Japan," said the little girl.

"What do they want?" said Potgieter.

"You!" said the little girl.

"You you!" said the third boy.

As they came around the first house and into the little square, where the women sold mangoes and onions and bananas, Potgieter saw the whole village gathered around the six Japanese soldiers and their sergeant. The priest and another man were nodding and pointing at the jeep, the headman stood next to the sergeant, gesturing up an alley, in the direction of Potgieter's house, three of the village dogs were trying to sniff the soldiers' boots and the children were laughing and shrieking, trying to keep the dogs away. Airlan stood with his arms folded, behind the jeep. At the back of the crowd stood the fat woman, a plump black chicken hanging from either hand. He didn't see Nyoman.

When the rest of the children saw Potgieter they left off chasing the dogs and rushed over to him, grasping at his hand and elbow or moving behind him to push his legs and his behind, push him toward the Japanese though he walked of his own accord.

The sergeant stepped out of the crowd and the soldiers formed a rank behind him. All of them looked pale and shaky, and the sergeant in particular looked to be on the verge of fainting.

"From Dutch?" said the sergeant wearily, in Dutch.

"Yes," said Potgieter. He had not spoken Dutch in a long time. "But I live in this village." He pointed down at the dusty red ground and two of the children mimicked him, pointing down at the ground as well.

The sergeant took a step forward and seized Potgieter by the wrist. The soldiers moved out of the way, and the sergeant led him to the jeep, releasing his arm and motioning for him to climb into the back. Then Jata appeared, standing between Potgieter and the sergeant, her arms out to keep the sergeant away, but the soldiers stepped in and knocked her back, and Potgieter stepped up into the jeep. It happened very quickly. Potgieter sat in his sarong with his hands on his knees and Jata lay on the ground, crying through her brown teeth. Then the fat woman stepped up and knocked one of the soldiers across the back of the head with her two chickens so his helmet came off, and the sergeant squawked an order and one of the soldiers slid behind the wheel, the sergeant into the other seat.

Then it flitted through Potgieter's mind what a fine painting this scene would make, so full of colour and activity, the Balinese all in yellows and reds, the Japanese in their uniforms of drab beige, the dogs and children scrambling around everyone's knees, the morning light glancing off the bayonets and the windshield and playing across the faces of the crowd, the soldiers, himself. A few of the women crying, screaming. Some of the men's faces grim, even bored. It was a well-set scene, like Rembrandt's *Night Watch*. A famous painting.

The jeep moved out of the village and the soldiers jogged after it two by two, and everyone was yelling something but Potgieter couldn't comprehend any of it. He saw the little crowd close around Jata and the children and dogs came running after the jeep, after the soldiers, then he was past the last house and out of the village.

They were under the palms then, moving along the wagon track that had never known an automobile before that day, and the air moving past Potgieter felt cool and dry, as it had never felt in years. But he still felt the nausea.

This is the end of things, then, thought Potgieter. The

Japanese had come after all and he was leaving the village behind. And the worst of it: the Japanese had come and Dalem had let them, had given Potgieter no word of warning. Had not spirited him away.

The soldiers trotting behind the jeep stared straight ahead, gripping their rifles tight in both hands. They looked ill. It occurred to him that their assignment was simply to travel from one village to another, collecting wayward Dutchmen. Because the Dutch are a militaristic people, empire-builders, a threat.

"I'm not from Dutch!" shouted Potgieter, and veins stood out on his sweating forehead. "I'm from that village! I'm not from Dutch!" He tried to stand, shouting out nonsense, putting out his arms to steady himself. The sergeant took his pistol from its holster, turned, reached up and struck Potgieter across the mouth with the handle of the gun, then the shoulder, then the chest, clubbing him. Potgieter's head snapped back, his hands flew up to cover his wounded mouth, and he dropped back into his seat. The sergeant gazed at him for a moment then faced forward again. Potgieter's teeth felt loose, jarred, and a little blood dripped down onto the sarong.

Across the padis to the east he saw a horse cantering steadily along an embankment, then stopping, stepping down onto the next wall, carefully making its way overland to the village. A brown figure sat upright on its back, so intent on the village it saw nothing on the road, didn't for an instant look that way.

Potgieter stared for a long time at the horse's shimmering flank.

"Do they speak Dutch in this village of yours?" said Cornelius. He was one of the men who had given Potgieter a ride south to Denpasar so many years before, the one who had smoked a pipe. The Japanese had taken his pipe away, though, so now he always had a twig in the corner of his mouth. Potgieter had recognized him immediately but Cornelius had not recognized Potgieter, though he did smile when he remembered giving a painter a ride to Denpasar.

"One of them speaks a little," said Potgieter. He turned the letter over and with the last of the ink in Cornelius's fountain pen began to carefully write the name of the village in swirling Balinese script.

"You can write Balinese!" said Cornelius, taking the twig out and placing it in the other corner of his mouth. "That's very impressive. I mean, we were in the service for years, but we, we had so much to do, you know, you couldn't absorb everything all at once."

"I can only write the one word," said Potgieter. "But I can recognize most of the words, on walls around the temple——."

"And they can read Dutch in your village too?"

"Read it? No, I don't think that anyone can."

"Oh, I see," said Cornelius.

Potgieter unfolded the letter and looked it over again. It was written entirely in Dutch.

Dear Dalem,

I am sorry I missed you at the village. If your father was not happy to see you I want you to live in my house. I will be back there soon. I have met some Dutch men and they say the Japanese will not be in the Indies for long, the Dutch will soon drive them out. I am in Sanur now, near Denpasar. I did not realize how many Dutch people were still in Bali. There are 200 or more. They are putting us on a ship. One Dutch man told me we are going to Pare-Pare, another told me to Celebes, I think maybe Pare-Pare is on Celebes. I will let you know when I get there. I miss you very much.

Yours sincerely,

Jan Potgieter

As they waited on the pier at Sanur some women came up from the beach, trying to sell handfuls of lichee-nut and wet slices of mango to the Dutchmen, who sat in a long line on the tarred planks. An old man with a hotel in Kuta had lent Potgieter some money. As one of the women shuffled along the pier, holding a handful of fruit above the men's heads, a full basket of mangoes balanced on her own, Potgieter smiled up at her, showing the gap where his tooth had been knocked out, and revealed the coins lying in his palm. She stooped down in front of him.

He took some mango, and with his free hand pulled the letter from the waist of his sarong and pressed it into her hand with the coins. She slid the letter into her basket, straightened up and moved along the line. The nearest soldier was only a few yards away, his back to them.

The woman did her best; she gave the letter to her sister-in-law, who was headed to the market at Denpasar with the eight tuna she had to sell.

"This is Dutch," said the sister-in law, unfolding the letter and peering at it.

"I know," said the woman.

"I have told you," said the sister-in-law, sighing, "that we don't work for them anymore. Every day I have to tell you that."

"They're good-looking, though, some of them," said the woman.

"Where are they going? Celebes? That boat won't make it to Celebes," said the sister-in-law.

"I've seen better," said the woman.

The sister-in-law had not heard of the village, but she was sure that someone at the big market in Denpasar would have. She carried it around a dozen stalls but everyone just shrugged, until finally a middle-aged man with a faint moustache told her he thought the village was near Ubud, up in the mountains. He was going in that direction in a few weeks' time to pick up his sister and take her to the festival in Gianyar, where their mother had been born. Why did people have to move around so much? The man shook his head.

Before Batubulan the letter flew off the seat of the man's cart and stuck on the branch of a tree. His two bullocks were very young and he didn't trust them not to run away while he retrieved the letter, and because there was a ditch near the tree he couldn't drive his cart underneath it. So he waited for nearly an hour until an old woman came along with a bamboo over her shoulder, so long that either end bumped against the ground. He called to her and she held the reins while he hopped down from the cart and pulled the letter off the tree. The woman could not have retrieved the letter herself because she was too short.

"How long did you wait? A long time?" said the old woman.

"Not so long," said the man. "Thank you, Mother."

"All right, all right," said the old woman, bowing her head a little. "All right, all right."

"What do you think of these Japanese?" said the man.

"They're better than the damn Dutch, aren't they?" She made a fist. "They beat the pants off of those Dutch!"

As he rode away the man considered what a good joke that was, because the Dutch always wore a pair of pants, never a sarong, and this was one of the differences that showed they didn't belong on Bali. Then again, the Japanese always wore trousers as well. He wondered if the old woman had thought of that.

In Batubulan the man met a troupe of Barong dancers travelling north to Ubud. Most of the dancers were on foot, but the huge shaggy head of the Barong costume sat in the back of a cart, and because of the way its terrible eyes seemed to twinkle at the man he quickly passed the letter off and was on his way. Afterwards he thought that he'd been silly to have been frightened, but his sister told him that the Barong had always given her nightmares. She told him that the idea of the Barong head riding in the back of a cart was absolutely terrifying, and the man smiled. He loved his sister.

The dancer who carried the letter didn't recognize the name of the village, but she thought the writing on the front was probably in Dutch. She didn't know any Dutch people in Ubud, but she knew a man from England lived there.

It was the next afternoon when the troupe walked into town, and the dancer went straight to the Englishman's house, through the gate and into the compound. But there was no-one there. She walked through the house and called out a few times, but everyone had gone. So she put the letter on the shrine in the courtyard, atop a film of dry and disintegrating blossoms. Someone who knows that village will come along sooner or later, she thought, and send it on its way.

She went out of the gate and ran to catch up with the others. She was dancing the Legong that night and would have to have her eyebrows plucked.

My Romance

Douglas Glover

Our boy Neddy died when he was three months old. I hardly remember any of this except for the brief hours following his birth when we were a normal, happy couple and then afterwards when Annie would wake in the night, choked with sobs, her milk streaming through the cloth of her nightgown. "My baby is hungry. He needs to eat," she would whisper, then collapse in a tight, convulsive ball, a rictus of despair.

When I heard her weeping like that, I wondered how anyone could live through such sadness. The look in her wild eyes pleaded with me to save her, to wake her from the nightmare, but all I could think of was holding him those first moments, dancing him a little in the delivery-room, peering into his dark blue eyes, crooning, "Neddy, Neddy, Neddy."

Afterwards I stopped sleeping. I made myself sit in his nursery with the dinosaur wallpaper I had put up, the little crib with the delicate white-painted spindles, the Babar poster, the musical mobile with the panda bears and stars that played Twinkle, twinkle, little star when you wound it up.

I drank neat bourbon, knocked back the Valium my doctor had given me, and smoked cigarettes. Sometimes I would pass out, but I never slept. "My baby is hungry," I heard her whisper. I couldn't go back into our bedroom when she was like that. The grief drove us apart. We were drowning in separate wells. Neddy never actually slept in the nursery. The nursery was all future. He slept in bed with us, tucked between us. Without saying a word, we both believed we could save him with the power of our love. That's when I stopped sleeping.

Afterwards, in the nursery, I got so that I would burn myself with cigarettes. I couldn't feel anything, but I wanted to see if I could feel anything, if feeling would ever come back.

"What are you doing, sweetheart?" she cried once when she found me like that.

I couldn't say. I was surprised she even noticed. I was playing Twinkle, twinkle, little star, watching the bears and stars circle above the place where Ned would have slept. The room smelled of singed hair and burnt skin.

She said, "I came to get the baby. I heard him crying. You know I can hear him quite well from the bedroom. He needs me. He needs to be fed."

She smelled sour from the old milk on her nightgown. Her breasts were huge and bountiful and useless. "You shouldn't smoke in here," she said sternly.

"He's dead," I said, sobbing so hard I couldn't catch my breath.

I was so lonely. At the same time, I was envious of her. She had slipped right out of herself into some fantasy. I remembered the afternoon we made Ned, the orange indicator on the ovulation test kit, our single-minded love, the sex without fear, the exhilaration of leaping into the future together. We looked into each other's eyes the whole time, until I came and my eyelids slid shut and I sank onto her shoulder and she held me. Now, even when we were in the same room talking, we were never together.

Part of me knew we were play-acting, cheering ourselves up. I understood that we were performing ancient rituals of grief. At the edge of the abyss you dance or you fall in. I

143

didn't really believe Annie thought she heard Neddy's cries in the night. This was her way of creating drama out of her heartsickness just as burning myself with cigarettes and drinking bourbon was my way of passing time that was otherwise utterly empty. It was the chilled emptiness we had fallen into which we could not abide and yet out of which we could not climb.

I remembered everything, of course: the first intimations of disaster, the falling weight, Neddy's constant whimpering cry, his bluish pallor, the blue haloes around his eyes, his lassitude, his chilliness against my skin. The doctor had a phrase for this—failure to thrive. She couldn't choose the words, they were all she had.

She was young and tall. I had never met anyone I could call willowy before I knew Dr. Tithonous. In better times, in her examining-room, she had charmed us with a little dance she did, miming with her hands the finger-like fimbria harvesting the eggs, her undulating body representing the Fallopian tubes. The fimbria dance. When she told us the bad news about Ned, she broke down herself, her long, pale hair fanning out over the cluttered desk as her head went down on her hands.

Annie and I were a little shocked at this show of emotion in a comparative stranger. After all Annie was holding Neddy on her lap, and he was still alive, if somewhat blue, and we couldn't quite credit the words of this overwrought woman across the desk. She said they called it failure to thrive. But I remembered reading in old books other phrases—mysterious wasting sickness, for example—which seemed more apt, more tied to the inexplicable nature of things.

It was as if Neddy, having come into the world, never quite managed to get a first grip on existence. His whole short life was an inexorable slipping back whence he had come. It made you think: What is life and what is death? Is there such a thing as being half-alive, tentatively alive? The darkness spewed him out, then sucked him back as if cancelling an error. I don't think he felt joy—he had a wry, flickering smile that would play across his face from time to time. And his whimpering signalled discomfort, not grief. I sometimes thought it might not have been so bad if he had lived a little, lived in the metaphorical sense—suffered joy and pain, raged and laughed. But he only lingered.

Oddly, the night Neddy died Annie and I both managed to sleep. We cradled his cool body between us on the bed, mashed our hot faces together and wept and wept and then slept. Nature is merciful, I think. They say that small animals go into a kind of anaesthetic shock as predators tear them to pieces. We didn't believe it was over, but something in us knew what had happened and yet briefly allowed us more than the usual fantasy of hope. We were momentarily together in a travesty of the togetherness we had felt a year before, making love, making Neddy.

There was some terrible irony in this, which neither of us understood. We could not put names or explanations to the contradictory emotions we felt. With a feeling that was sometimes uncomfortably close to embarrassment, we had lost all sense of who we really were. Everything was tasteless, colourless. Words were meaningless. We told each other "I love you" because we both had a vestigial, somewhat dutiful, impulse to comfort one another. We remembered, as if in a dream, that other time when we were really together. But we both also knew these were empty words.

Language is a machine of desire. It works along an axis defined by hope and future. When there is no hope and future, the mysterious bonds of syntax, the wires that convey the energy of meaning from word to word, disintegrate. Words become snarls, shrieks and gurgles of despair or they become rituals, motions you go through to pass the time, to try to cheer yourself up. If I say "I love you" enough times, perhaps I will remember what that felt like, what the words mean. But the truth is all I remember is how cold Neddy was, lying between us that morning when we woke up and I reached for the telephone to call Dr. Tithonous.

Of course, at that time of day, I only got her service. My voice was breaking. I could only croak out the words. I said, "Please tell Barbara"—I had never used her first name before—"please tell her Neddy died in the night that we're here with him in the bed that we can't leave him that we don't know what to do now and could she please help us."

You expect the operators at the answering service to be distant and business-like at best, or cold and nasty at worst. But this one seemed, through some miracle of wire and electrons, to understand every nuance of what I was saying. Her voice came back to me kindly and sorrowful. "Sir, I want you to know I will call Dr. Tithonous as soon as you hang up. I'll call her till I find her. I don't want you to worry about this. I'll get someone there right away."

She knew she couldn't help me much, but she wanted me to be sure she would do everything she could. And she didn't offer to do more. She didn't say goodbye.

Almost as soon as I hung up, the phone rang and it was Dr. Tithonous. "Jack, I am just calling to let you know I am driving right over myself. I wanted you not to worry."

It broke my heart a second time to have these people trying to take care of us, being so kind. All the protocols and stereotypes were breaking down. Out of all the wretchedness came the distant mutterings of the human heart. I did not think this then, only later. At the time I only felt an unreasonable relief and turned to try to cuddle little Neddy one last time, to try to pretend he was alive. And then, moments later, it seemed, I heard the doorbell and stumbled out into the living-room in my pyjamas.

Dr. Tithonous embraced me at the door, just held me, for an eternity, it seemed. I felt her dry sobs catch on my ear. Then she let me go and strode quickly into the bedroom. She was wearing faded jeans and a man's shirt not tucked in properly, evidence of her haste in coming. Her hair was still in disarray from sleep. She knelt beside Annie, stroked her hair and whispered to her. I don't know what she said.

Annie had the baby at her breast. Her breasts were bare, distended, ready to burst. Milk had spurted out over the sheets, pooled on her belly. Dr. Tithonous cradled her head and whispered. She touched my wife's breasts, she kissed her temples, she felt the baby's cheek with the back of her hand. At that moment, she seemed to shudder and she buried her eyes briefly against Annie's shoulder.

I caught sight of myself in Annie's full-length mirror against the closet door. Eyes like dark stones, mouth hanging open. I had an erection, I suddenly noticed. The wild incongruity of this almost drove me to my knees. And I could not think about it then, thought about it later in my bourbon and valium stupor, when I could only wonder at the mysterious and paradoxical messages ripping through my heart at that moment, as if I were somehow completely separate from those things called "Jack" and "body" and "self" or as if I had suddenly become a centre for all meanings and impulses at once.

In that strange moment, I had the distinct impression that I was either more myself than I had ever been or completely separate from myself, and there was no difference between these states, because the self I was or wasn't seemed more utterly alien and mysterious to me than anything I had ever experienced. Finally I crawled into bed with my wife and dead baby, with my erection, in a gross and humiliating parody of the moment of conception, when, yes, we were all together, too. And Dr. Tithonous stayed with us in the death room, in this state of barbaric intimacy.

Weeks later it is like this: I tell Annie I am going to play golf. I don't even bother to put my clubs in the trunk. They sit there in the garage behind the infant car seat neither of us can bear to move or give away. If Annie looked, she would know that I am not playing golf. I don't know if she looks, she never says a word. I just tell her. The Canada geese have come and gone, snow flurries fall—still I head out to play golf with obsessive regularity. What is Annie thinking?

I drive out Route 9 to a little motel called the Royal which climbs up a shattered limestone ridge and hangs in a state of instability and tension with the scrub pine, sumac and poison ivy tumbling down the steep slopes. Dr. Tithonous meets me there when she can break away from her patients. I wait for her in one of the guest cottages, sipping Old Crow from a Dixie cup. Sometimes I fall asleep. The guest cottages at the Royal are the only place I can sleep these days. Often I wake up to find Barbara tucked up beside me wearing nothing but her bra and underpants, her cell phone and beeper placed neatly upon the bedside table next to the lamp and digital alarm clock radio.

What happens next is difficult to relate. One's deepest desires are always paradoxical and humiliating. You go there as into some dark vortex at the bottom of which is death which seems, in this aspect, breathtakingly sweet. Or put it this way: sex is inextricably entwined with desire, wanting, but what we want is not always sex. Sometimes we desire pure desire, the endless wanting whose only end is the extinction of itself, that point of voluptuous rest from wanting. Or we crave some reminder or replica of the utter desperation of life, the way it eats itself up, the self-destructiveness of it all. So it is all desperate, whispered entreaties, whimpered protests, grunts, moans and cries in the dark. I can guess why I am there but what secret sadness drives Barbara to the Royal Motel I cannot tell. I cannot connect the face of the dancer who showed us with her body the ancient processes of nature with the lover who begs me to perform the filthiest, most unseemly acts, who only cries out for rest so that she can reach some stranger ecstasy.

Once she told me the story of her life (it is my opinion we all have, at most, only one or two stories to tell), how she had married another doctor named East, how he left her the year he did eight ultrasounds on a pregnant woman and missed the fact that her baby had no brain, how the year Dr. East left, Barbara's twin sister Miranda died of leukemia. Near the end, Barbara came often to sit by her bedside, spelling their exhausted, heartsick parents. One night Miranda woke, vomiting, from a drugged slumber. Unable to quell the spasms, even to catch her breath, she threw herself off the bed in agony, and crouched trembling on the floor like an animal, horrid blasts of air and fluid shooting up her esophagus and out her anus, tears, sweat and spit spattering the carpet. She cried, over and over, "I'm dying, Barbie. I'm dying."

"She wanted me to leave. She was terrified. Her voice sounded like a little girl's. But it was all her own, the dying consumed her, she wanted to be alone. Her body was ripping itself apart, but she didn't want help or comfort. She wanted me to leave so I wouldn't distract her from the dying. She was tired of caring for people. What does that mean? I'm a doctor, but I don't know what it means. That year everyone abandoned me."

"The trouble with modern medicine," I tell her, "is that it has simply extended human life-expectancy twenty or thirty years into the limbo of anti-climax—not something Neddy had to worry about either."

We both flinch at the sound of Neddy's name, though we both also know that if I didn't just keep talking like this I'd have no recourse but to beat my brains out with one of the white-washed rocks lining the parking-pad outside the cottage.

She says, "What modern medicine has taught me is that experience is suffering, and most of the time we have drugs for that."

Beyond the limestone ridge lies a tract of wild country called the Devil's Den. Bobcats haunt the tangled undergrowth, maybe a bear, plenty of deer, the motel owner tells me. The motel owner's name is Ben, and he lives with his wife Marge who hacks around the diminutive owner's suite with a tank of oxygen on a little cart and a mask over her face. Ben smokes in the breezeway by the neon sign that says OFFICE. He wears his long white hair pulled back in a ponytail so tight it seems to drag the skin of his bony face into a mask.

Ben and Marge have a son named Mike who lives in exile in one of the guest cottages. Ben says Mike's a loner which is short for a divorced part-time woodcutter who spends most of his time gambling at the harness track or riding around the Devil's Den on his four-wheel ATV, getting drunk. They also have a Brazilian grey monkey named Michael, which they keep in a large cage in Mike's former bedroom in the owner's suite. Ben and Marge think this thin domestic joke is hilarious.

We are all accomplices, it seems. We will do almost anything, enact any cruelty, to keep from thinking about what we are not thinking about. And this strange antithesis of a romance which Dr. Tithonous and I prosecute in the little housekeeping cabin beneath the Devil's Den is nothing but a trick and a sign of what it is not. It would be a mistake to think that we are sad precisely. It is closer to the truth to imagine Barbara, Annie and I (and Ben and Marge and Mike) pursuing our dark ecstasies with a certain rueful zest—after all, we are not the ones who died, yet. Having watched Neddy slip out of the mist and then drift quietly back into the mist—always the mystery of the sweet half-smile—we lurch backward from the edge with a sharpened sense of self, of the pathos of our brief theatrics. The sounds Dr. Tithonous makes during sex are almost indescribable (as were the sounds her sister made grappling with her death). They haunt me still.

I tell you this mainly because it makes me feel better. It's not worth speaking about otherwise. Language is 80% consolation, 20% aphrodisiac. Communication is an outmoded enterprise, honesty a fake, love a conservative political agenda. Sex is the only thing you can't sell anymore, a baroque topological assault upon the envelope of the soul, a form of prayer. All the orifices are good because they get you closer to God. The only sense of self left to us is the sense of the self as actor, that is, when we are pretending to be someone else—hence the ruinous cult of Hollywood celebrity. It is as if we have been inoculated with that same mysterious wasting sickness, contaminated with death.

One day when Barbara and I are in the throes of something or other, her beeper sounds. She shrugs her shirt and jeans over her pale, bruised body. Her lips are bleeding, her breasts are palimpsests of bruises fading from black to gold. She seems faintly noble, if not heroic, buttoning herself, tossing her long hair over her shoulders, staggering out past the shuttered windows into the blazing sunlight. Her lips wear a thin, rueful smile, the twin of Neddy's.

Left alone, I smoke a cigarette and take inventory, wondering if, this time, we have done anything irrevocable. But almost at once I fall prey to remembering, to my ineluctable past, to visions of empty nurseries, abandoned car seats, my wife's seeping breasts, her night cries: memories which inevitably drive me out in search of further distraction. How can you sit alone after you've heard those words? "My baby is hungry. He needs to eat."

Outside Mike is packing cans of beer into saddlebags in preparation for his version of a nature hike, a jaunt through the Devil's Den on his ATV. I watch him in silence, but the silence only compels me to engage him in conversation, to make some claim on existence through the sound of my own voice. I tell Mike this thing with Neddy has put me in a state. I ask him if he thinks Annie has the moral edge on me because she just sits in the nursery weeping, zonked on Zoloft and Restoril she gets from Dr. Tithonous. I tell him I can't stand to be with her, that I am scared to death of really feeling as bad as I feel, that she only reminds me of that. When I'm in that room with her, I say, I think I might have to kill her to get through this, kill her and then call in an air strike and nuke the nursery, the house, the yard (with that swingset I bought as a kit and spent a weekend putting together), the whole damn city and let loose a cloud of radiation that circumnavigates the globe killing everything else.

Mike says, "Right."

He says very little at the best of times but generally knows exactly how to calm me down. I know he has his own family issues. Ben is always looking at Marge's oxygen tank and cart and saying things like, "Can't wait till we get that shit out of the house." And Marge has told me with some enthusiasm that Ben has an aneurysm, that he'll probably die the next time he sneezes. They both tell me they made a will giving the motel to the Brazilian grey monkey instead of Mike, though they made Mike the executor. They despise Mike for some obscure failure, some purely human thing, I suspect.

Mike himself traces it back to when he was six and his guinea pig Pinky died and he cried too much. He says Ben felt so bad that he couldn't fix things that he decided to blame Mike. "He decided I was a wimp and a cry-baby," says Mike. "I've been a flop ever since."

I tell him it's a fundamental human trait to be inhuman to other humans. And then I say, "Maybe it's a kind of love, you know, not wanting to disrupt your father's view of things."

Mike says, "Right."

And then he says, "You want to go into the Den and raise hell?"

And I say, "I'm in the mood to drive all the way to the

bottom and kick Beelzebub in the nuts."

We climb past the deer lick where Mike puts out corn and salt through the winter, through a narrow gorge along an old logging road as far as a row of water-filled caves cut into the side of a hill, a former graphite mine abandoned at the turn of the century. A cold wind blows steadily out of those caves. The soft rock above the gaping entries seems ready to fall at any moment. They could be the gates of Hell. Mike says a hunter disappeared into those caves once, going after a dog that fell through the ice early one spring.

We drink beer, sitting back to back against a young oak growing up from the top of a ridge of mine tailings.

"We're sitting on history," Mike says, though I have never known him to wax philosophical, and I take it as a sign of advanced drunkenness. I myself can't stop thinking about our earlier conversation.

I say, "I don't think there is any such thing as love, or love is just humoring the other person, not wanting to disrupt her vision of things."

"Two people humoring each other?" Mike asks.

"No," I say, "I don't think it works like that. One or the other." And then I add, "I think people can't stand to be in love, that it makes them nervous, that they try to wreck it because the memory of love is everlasting whereas love itself is always fleeting. I read in the paper about this new condition called reactive attachment disorder where people keep themselves in constant physical pain to ward off the larger emotional pain of the loss of love. Now no-one said they were going to lose love, but they might. It's the terrible thought that love might end that pushes people to destroy love and themselves."

"That's probably what I've got," says Mike. "I had it before they invented it," he says.

He pulls a .357 handgun from his saddlebag, and we take turns potting the trees. I am a terrible shot, but Mike can nip the twigs off branches. We shoot and shoot, and when we run out of bullets, a litter of fresh-fallen twigs and leaves lies about us.

We pack up and head back down to the Royal. Mike fetches a fresh clip from his cabin and, for no reason at all except that it seems like a good idea, we head over to the owner's suite. Ben is away, Marge is sleeping, snoring into her oxygen mask. We sneak into his old bedroom where Michael, the Brazilian grey monkey, darts up at the sound of visitors. The sweet smell of pine chips and rotting fruit, mixed with the acidic tang of old monkey piss, rises from the floor of his cage. A pennant from Niagara Falls, a KISS poster and a plastic dream-catcher adorn the oddly Spartan walls. A plastic ME-109, built from a kit, swings on a length of fishing line. But there is no furniture, just the cage.

For some reason, I think the room is an image of the inside of my mind, or Mike's mind. I am almost too drunk to know which is which. Mike holds the pistol to Michael's head. The monkey, after his initial enthusiasm, has lapsed into apathetic torpor. He squats on the floor of the cage, flipping his flaccid, worm-like penis back and forth with the back of his hand. He peers at the gun without any discernible interest, and then, as if understanding what's to come, places his other hand over his eyes, the long fingers seeming to stretch almost half-way around his head. His long, skinny limbs make him look oddly insect-like, but the overall effect—the steel bars, the flapping penis, the awkward crouch—is one of pathos, of things not in their right place, of interminable anxiety.

I feel a thrill of dread, an almost delicious anticipation of some terrible climax toward which the day or my whole life has been tending. The smell from the cage or the vision of monkey brains soaking into the pine chips makes me gag. But I cannot tear myself away. I am already worried that this will end too soon, that Mike and I will run out of interesting things to do for the rest of the afternoon. I am dying, Annie, I think. I am dying.

But then, as if the whole thing had been a whim, Mike lowers the barrel of the gun, feels with his fingertips above the door lintel for a key, unlocks the cage and grabs Michael by the scruff of his neck. One-handed he slides open a window which looks out upon the trail going up to Devil's Den. I can just see the deer lick 200 yards into the woods, the limestone walls of the gorge poking out of the pines. Mike kicks the screen out of the window and heaves the monkey into the yard. Michael falls in a dusty heap, then resumes his apathetic squat.

But it is cold out there, the chill wind (it seems to come down from those caves, seems to be following us) ruffles his fur. The monkey peers about, then squints at us watching him from the window. You can see questions beginning to form, warring with years of habit, boredom and loneliness. He dabs at the dry pine needles with his fingertips, watches a handful fly away in the breeze. He faces the wind coming over the Devil's Den, and suddenly the shadows within his eyes deepen as if opening into a long-locked room.

The wind in his fur gives him that ancient warrior look. What this really means I don't know. And I was drunk. Perhaps all meaning is context, or perhaps I was simply prey to the hormones flushing through my system, my lost paternity. But I saw him so. Mike's reaction is to drop to his knees, cradle his shooting arm against the window-sill and take aim. A ball of terror collects in my stomach.

Mike aims, fires. But the bullet flies wide. The monkey's head snaps around, his suspicious eyes absorbing the picture of the two men and the gun, none of which he understands. But some intuition, some reserve of instinct warns him—the air seems suddenly to thicken around us. And he begins an easy four-legged lope up the hillside.

Mike blasts away till his clip is empty. His face glows crimson above his collar, his gun-hand trembles crazily as if some invisible being were struggling to wrest the gun away from him. He looks beaten, defeated, or like a man about to have a stroke. He shouldn't have missed. I wonder why he did. The monkey pauses at the deer lick, squats again, cranes his neck to look first up the trail and then back down at us. He is clearly uncertain about the future, about bobcats and the cold. But uncertainty holds him only a moment, and the monkey bravely resumes his upward journey in the direction of who knows what bloody future hurtling toward him.

"He'll be dead in a week," says Mike, breathing heavily, watching the wispy grey fur of the monkey's back disappear into the trees. "If the cats don't get him, he'll starve to death."

Mike starts to laugh. It's as if he starts, then pauses a moment to see what it feels like to laugh at this juncture, then continues, the volume rising in waves. I can't tell if this is an act or not. Perhaps the whole thing has been an act. Or perhaps there are good reasons for Marge and Ben to keep their son in one of the farther cottages. His face looks like the head of a match bursting into flame.

I can only think how heroic the monkey looks in contrast to his human brother, how satisfying a prospect his night of freedom and violent death seems. And I ponder the mystery of that judgment. This is the old romantic trap, I think. In what sense can it be true that the monkey's brief, sweet sojourn in the Den can be more real, more authentic, than life in a warm cage?

I am sick in bed for three days after this bout of drunkenness (what my father used to call a toot), but it wakes me up, wakes up my moral being. I once thought you could get through anything by striking attitudes and spouting a little philosophy. But that's not true. I am not going to get through this, and what I am doing with Dr. Tithonous is wrong. I mean I am going to get through it. I am alive after all. But my life has changed irrevocably. The person I am now and the person I was before Neddy died are discontinuous, though related, like second cousins once removed. My new self is a 90-year-old man with whom I have difficulty relating or even communicating.

On top of everything else, I decide my marriage is coming apart. Little indications of seismic upheaval abound: the way Annie drifts out of rooms as I enter, the sound of uncontrollable sobbing behind locked doors and her perfect composure when she actually appears, her sudden interest in therapy and her reconnection with an old girlfriend named Rosellen who recently moved back to the city. There is nothing definite, only an incremental decline, a mysterious wasting.

Annie knows nothing of my affair with Dr. Tithonous, but she accuses me with her eyes when she thinks I am not looking. These silent accusations are troubling in their implication. What betrayal am I being charged with? Did I wish Neddy dead? Am I taking it all too lightly with my endless golf-playing? What can she think? To me, her anger seems gratuitous, its own species of betrayal. Does she think I actually want to act the way I am acting, that I have any control? I stopped getting what I wanted the moment Neddy died. Everything since then can only be described as fate or gesture. Am I really to be blamed because I am no less capable than she of bridging the silence between us?

Not that there weren't signs of trouble before Neddy was born. Annie and I were both ambivalent, but we were both also tired of our dithering. So we went ahead and made the baby, and briefly the act of taking a risk restored to us our sense of adventure, brought us together as nothing else had since the very beginning of our relationship when likewise, impelled by panache and a willingness to gamble, we threw ourselves together. Character is action, action is fate. You are someone when you do something. The rest of the time you wallow. Life becomes this endless tension between wallowing and our little abortive attempts to compose a self through action. The polar modes of existence: wallowing and a desperate, mindless darting. Annie and I are just two normal, modern people caught in the soup—but she blames me for this. (In the East, of course, they order things differently—under a regime of quietism and self-abandonment, what we call character is merely an individual pathology. I am perfectly aware that all this frenzy of doing and anxiety may be completely beside the point, that we might only be perpetuating some ancient sacrificial mode.)

Annie and I met one summer between college terms, in a little café around the corner from the Rodin Museum in Paris. I was travelling alone. She was with her brother and his fiancée, a buxom Californian who resented having to drag Annie along wherever they went. I had watched them wander through the museum. The brother and his fiancée were clearly bored—they kissed in front of the Kiss, they held hands in front of the Hands, they leaned on each other in front of the Burghers of Calais. Annie looked forlorn, miserable. Her face was pale as if she hadn't slept. You actually had to look twice to see her beauty.

I followed them to the café, then made myself a nuisance, asking directions, folding my map out onto their table. I asked Annie to come with me for the afternoon. She said no. The fiancée urged her to have an adventure. You could see the look of relief flooding over all three faces. "You saved me from my version of a wicked stepmother," she said afterward, laughing. But, equally, she had saved me from a terrible loneliness and self-perpetuating insecurity. And her laughter had a forced quality to it as if she were trying to put the best face on things.

How this sense of uneasy relief and gratitude turned into love is a caution and a mystery. Perhaps it was only that we did not know what love was and mistook whatever it was we were feeling for love. Or that, both of us being unable to bear disappointment in the other, we manufactured an enthusiasm, which was otherwise lacking, in order to feast on the delight in the other's eyes. Hence the eerie emptiness, the silence which seemed always to surround our love, the sense that if we did not keep upping the ante, as it were, risking more, our love would disappear. This, it seems to me, is somehow the essence of romantic love, a love founded upon its own impossibility, a love which paradoxically feeds upon itself in order to grow.

Love is thus a disease of the will which creates a deformed double of itself as an instrument of desire. In time, the double, the lover, seems to attain a degree of reality greater than the original self—Annie and I both grew to feel left out of our marriage. Who were those two people fornicating so energetically, so joylessly, upon the counterpane? Not she, or me. Would Neddy have made us real again?

My new moral self, discovered after bottoming out and conspiring to murder a Brazilian grey monkey at the Royal Motel, decides to make a clean breast of things. Perhaps this is not a new moral self, perhaps it is only the old pathological self that just has to keep stirring things up in order to feel alive. It's difficult to tell. I meet Dr. Tithonous at the Royal and tell her I can't see her anymore. She tells me she isn't wearing any underwear, that there is dampness trickling down the insides of her thighs, that she has longed for this moment, the moment of rejection. Weeping, she falls to her knees and, fumbling with my belt, begs me desperately to make love to her, a locution she has never used in the past. She has become a glutton for humiliation. Why do I feel, once again, that we are acting out some universal drama, that poetics has turned into theatrics? Our obsession with one another is about to transform itself into shame and loathing on her side and mild distaste and irritation on mine. A week ago we were at each other like dogs in heat, and a week from now we'll both be wishing it had never happened. It's a wonder to me that the so-called experts haven't realized that we're all going around in a state of chronic low-grade schizophrenia, that identity is a fiction.

My new moral self drives home, with a certain self-righteous precision, and discovers Annie in the nursery, rocking almost imperceptibly in the little rocking-chair she meant to use for nursing Neddy, listening to the panda bear-and-stars mobile playing Twinkle, twinkle, little star. She's in there communing with our son, I think. But then again maybe she is in there communing with me—for this is now my favourite room in the house, the place where I spend my lonely hours. I smell of sex with Dr. Tithonous (my new moral self winces at this admission). Annie looks sad and pensive and suddenly more beautiful than I have ever seen her, as if after all the undignified suffering she has achieved some deeper knowledge of the meaning of things.

I had marched into the house full of hatred for myself and my wife, ready to slay her with my revelations, ready to demolish her with honesty for all that pathetic flailing about I hate in myself (so much for the new moral self—whenever you feel the moral self waking within, you can bet an act of injustice and inhumanity is about to follow). But she only glances up at me with a bemused, slightly embarrassed half-smile on her face which reminds me of nothing so much as Neddy, oh, these eons ago. For it was her smile I was seeing on his face, only I'd forgotten.

And all at once I feel such a welling up of love for Annie, love and passion and desire. My limbs tremble as contrary emotions surge through me. My eyes grow hot, heavy-lidded with tears. I remember the splendour of making Neddy. I recall the terrible hope in our hearts. I want just to touch her, and go on touching her for the rest of my life, to catch her hand and put my cheek against hers so that I might feel the warmth of her flesh and smell the sweetness of her breath as it goes in and out and remember, oh, remember what hope was like. There has never been anything else I ever wanted and nothing more I will ever want. I am completely undone, unstrung, helpless.

She says, "Hey, you." She touches my foot with hers and holds up her arms to pull me in. Her eyes are full of mischief, a weary merriment, irresistible eyes.

I hesitate because now I have a terrible truth to tell, something unforgivable that will come slamming down on us like a steel door, crushing this sudden afflatus of love like a delicate flower.

I call it love, for want of a better word—I don't know what it is really. Beyond us there is a void, and inside us there is a void. At the centre, the self is inscrutable. We ride the dark, lunar surfaces of unknown objects our whole lives long, we are receivers of messages the provenance of which is as obscure as death itself. It seems to test us, to drown us, grow us, betray us, destroy us. Before it, we are alone. And yet between the void and the shallow dogmas of psychotherapeutics there remains some residue, some faint sediment of what? The thing you can't see for looking at, the thing disappearing at the corner of your eye, the thing not conceived in any of your philosophies, the thing that is not the void and not the half-crazy, shambling beast of desire that dogs our lives (what the Buddhists call "the little self"). This is the place where love resides, if love resides.

I lay my head upon her lap. The rocking-chair is still. Annie strokes my temples, the nape of my neck, and, sobbing because my heart is brokenbrokenbroken, I tell her that our boy is dead, that this is the only real thing that's happened, that getting so close to reality is like putting your head in a giant wall socket, that every certainty has been upended, the linchpin knocked out of my life, the keystone dropped from the arch. I can't figure out how to take another step, but I wander on, embarrassed by my own seeming indestructibility. I can't say who is telling my feet to move. It's not me giving the orders. "I tried so hard," I sob. I don't know why my heart seems suddenly to break again when I say the words, "I tried so hard." But the tears are gushing out of me, my body is wracked with sadness.

The rhythm of Annie's caresses never falters. She says nothing. I feel the gentle insistence of the flesh of her thigh against my cheek, reminding me of her sexual presence, of our consequential passions. I think how my present prostration is the only correct response to the world, that if we could see the world the way it really is, there would be nothing but this weeping and biting of hands. I think, now I am where I belong.

But, presently, without looking into her face, I begin to tell Annie about my afternoons at the Royal Motel with Dr. Tithonous. (How many times, in the grip of some outré perversity, did I recall the vision of the doctor crouched beside the bed, whispering into Annie's ear, the soiled nightgown, the streaming breasts, both women mysteriously out of themselves, forgetful of me? How many times did I pity the doctor for her subterranean hungers? It seemed, yes, that she was the most tragic of us all, the one to whom science had revealed all secrets but who had drifted farthest from the truth. What is the truth? Once I told her, "Modern medicine is a crutch we should throw away." (Impossible to know what I meant.)

I can barely get the words out, but each sound uttered increases my confidence in the story. Somehow, I suppose, I'd thought that language would prove incapable of conveying the monstrous details, that I wouldn't be able to tell her. But the very miracle of turning my assignations into sentences and paragraphs has the odd effect of domesticating them, making them feel reasonable, part of the known world (another function of language: it renders everything it touches trivial and slightly seedy). I hadn't gone beyond the moon—I had met our pediatrician at a motel because I was upset about what happened to Neddy who died at three months of a mysterious wasting disease. This sounds so plausible, and Annie's response—silence—seems so benign, that I almost stop feeling guilty, though moments later my heart races with anxiety over the obvious discrepancies between my words and the facts, language's inadequacy as a device for communicating, signalled here by Annie's first words when she does begin to speak—something about a monkey, as if I have somehow mixed up the story about the monkey with the story about Dr. Tithonous.

Fresh reasons for despair—I can't even confess to my wife without inspiring a misunderstanding, without the words somehow being misconstrued. The thing is absolutely impossible—she can't see into my heart. Or have I simply been lying again without knowing it—the truth is I believe in fairies, talking animals and multiple personality disorders.

I repeat here that the only real thing that's happened is that Neddy died (all the rest—Annie crying, "My baby's hungry, I have to feed my baby," me burning myself with cigarettes in the nursery, my affair with Dr. Tithonous, the attempted murder of the monkey—all the rest is true too, but in the manner of a code or a substitute for the real thing). The sad thing is that part of me already no longer believes Neddy lived and died. The New Agers call this the healing process. Mourning has its rhythms and stages, and pretty soon it is as if the thing itself didn't happen, just the mourning and the healing. The aftermath becomes the thing—like the intergalactic radiation that remains our only evidence for the Big Bang at the beginning of Time. By substitution, by the metaphoric process of language, we move incrementally away from the edge of reality, back into the everyday zone of safety and lies—we ought to put a stop to healing, I think.

Annie gently asks again about the monkey. This time I have to look at her face to see if indeed she might not have gone completely insane (always a distinct possibility with human beings), but there is only that curious half-smile,

Neddy's smile, about which now I see I was mistaken. It's not uncertain, wan and etiolate, as I had thought. Rather it is a smile of affection, only slightly uncertain of response, waiting for a response. It occurs to me suddenly, blindingly, that Neddy loved us—that was the message of the smile—and that he knew he was loved.

This realization unleashes fresh storms of grief. I am a boy again sobbing inconsolably over the unfairness of life. I have never felt such pain and, simultaneously, such release—an access of fatigue and self-pity. Annie cradles my face against her breasts and begins to rock again ever so slightly.

All at once I am kissing her, struggling to undo the buttons of her shirt. She releases me slightly from our embrace to help. Her breasts are large, slightly under-inflated, as it were, as they begin to shrink back to their normal size. Flawed like this, they have never seemed more desirable. They tell me a story, something about the life of women. I suck them, tasting the thin, bittersweet taste of her milk. She rocks me, croons one of those children's songs she had been memorizing through her pregnancy. And soon we are making love on the floor, very carefully, very tenderly, without thinking about birth control, just the way we did when we made Neddy.

It is a strange sort of excitement, full of history and sadness, calm somehow, without the usual agitation of sexual desire. We look into each other's eyes and feel our bodies rising, but we are distant from that. The thing that is empty inside me is pouring itself into Annie, and into the minatory and morbid future.

Nothing makes sense. And it has stopped being a story. I have to fight to keep my anxiety for sense and explanations from corrupting the moment. The moment is already corrupt when I think that it doesn't make sense, for there is no perception without words. And there is no such thing as the things we call by the words "love" and "human being" and "soul." I can only hope that by some backwards logic that the moment that makes no sense somehow makes the most sense, that the truth is true because it is unrecognizable. In this moment, I also do not recognize myself or my wife. But I feel a surge of forgiveness and generosity flowing from her, out of the mysterious and alien emptiness that is all I can know of her. It has none of the conventional passion or even coziness of the thing we normally call love. All that has burned off with the loss of Neddy.

Momentarily, as we come back to ourselves, we are like tired, wounded soldiers, strangers to one another, supporting each other out of the battle. We cannot save each other, we cannot escape, but there is some human dignity to be claimed in the comradeship of the doomed. We hold each other, a little abashed at what we have done. And I can see the old pieties and anxieties beginning to reassert themselves in Annie's eyes. There is some hurt there now, the beginnings of resentment (the feeling of the age), though I can also see that she is fighting this, clearly surprised and proud of her spiritual daring.

I myself am startled by a sudden perception of Annie's mysterious depths, how different she is from any expectation I have of her, how she is herself, surprising and other. I cannot calculate the reasons for this, but where I could only think to touch her with my anger and violence, she has found a way to reach back with love and forgiveness. This gesture is transformative just as it is tentative and temporary. So much of what is good in life has this quality of fleetingness, a glimpse snatched through a closing door, an infant dying. But it makes me love her back, though I don't know what it means to say that.

Six months later they find Ben and Marge dead together in the bedroom, holding hands. There is a note that says they decided they could not live without each other and were afraid they would soon lose the chance to make that choice themselves. Suddenly Mike owns the Royal Motel. He stops drinking out of shock, not because his parents killed themselves but because of that note. "I thought they hated each other," he says. He thought they hated him too, and now his whole universe has been turned upside down.

I myself am puzzled by the violent shifting of things, the lack of continuity between words and actions. Nothing in their self-presentations had prepared me for the couple's dramatic liebestod. I say, "Mike, sometimes it seems as if life is designed specifically to demolish every certainty, every categorical statement. Or else it's a novel being written by a very bad and inattentive author who cannot even bother to keep the characters straight."

Since that fateful afternoon of violence, there has been no sign of the Brazilian grey monkey—no body, no tell-tale fur patches or crushed, half-eaten bones—it is as if he walked into the Devil's Den and disappeared. Mike, who has had a complete change of heart about the monkey and searches for him constantly (leaving little caches of monkey food among the rocks), believes the monkey just kept on walking and somehow is on his way back to Brazil, home.

MATT COHEN was born in Kingston and educated in Toronto. He taught for a time at McMaster and has been writer-in-residence at a number of other universities. His books include *The Disinherited*, *The Colours of War*, *The Sweet Second Summer of Kitty Malone* and *The Spanish Doctor*. A new collection of stories will be published next year.

LIBBY CREELMAN was born in Cambridge, Massachusetts and has lived in St. John's, Newfoundland since 1983. Her stories have been published in *TickleAce*, *The Fiddlehead*, *Pottersfield Portfolio*, *The New Quarterly* and the *Journey Prize Anthology*. A collection of short stories is forthcoming.

BRUCE MCCALL was born and raised in Simcoe, Ontario. He moved to New York City in 1965 and has lived there ever since, working as a humorous writer and illustrator for such publications as *The New Yorker* and *Vanity Fair*. One of his two published books, *Thin Ice*, is a memoir of his Canadian upbringing and he remains a Canadian citizen.

JANE EATON HAMILTON is the author of four books, including *July Nights*, a collection of stories. She has won the *Prism International*, *This Magazine*, *Event*, *Belles Lettres* and *Yellow Silk* awards and the Canadian Chapbook Competition. Her stories have been cited for *Best American Short Stories* and the Pushcart Prize and appeared in places as varied as the *New York Times* and *Seventeen* magazine.

MIKE BARNES has published poems and stories in numerous magazines including *The New Quarterly*, *Descant*, *The Malahat Review*, *The Fiddlehead*, *Dandelion* and *Blood & Aphorisms*. His collection of poems, *Calm Jazz Sea*, was published by Brick Books in 1996 and shortlisted for the Gerald Lampert Memorial Award. A story collection, *Aquarium*, will appear in the fall of 1999.

FRANÇOIS BONNEVILLE was born in Halifax and raised in Quebec City and in Boston, Massachusetts, where his father worked for NASA. He has lived all over North America, studied creative writing in Colorado and at the University of British Columbia, and spent a year writing in France. In 1998 he published a memoir of his wife's battle with depression, *My Years of Her Melancholy*.

MADELEINE THIEN has published stories in *Event*, *The Fiddlehead* and the *Journey Prize Anthology*. She has been shortlisted for the CBC Literary Award and the Bronwen Wallace Prize, and her collection-in-progress, *Simple Recipes and Other Stories*, recently won the Asian-Canadian Writers' Workshop Emerging Writer Award. She lives in Vancouver where she is beginning a Masters degree at UBC.

ADAM LEWIS SCHROEDER grew up in Vernon, BC, and now lives in Vancouver, where he works at the hostel on Jericho Beach. His stories have appeared in *Zygote*, *Grain* and Scribner's *Best of the Fiction Workshops*. He is currently working on a story collection and a western screenplay set in British Columbia.

DOUGLAS GLOVER is the author of three story collections and three novels, including the critically acclaimed *The Life and Times of Captain N*. His stories have appeared in *Best American Short Stories*, *Best Canadian Stories* and *The New Oxford Book of Canadian Stories*, and criticism has appeared in the *Globe and Mail*, *Montreal Gazette*, *New York Times Book Review*, *Washington Post Book World* and *Los Angeles Times*. A collection of his essays, *Notes Home from a Prodigal Son*, will be published this fall.